Novels by Chico Buarque

Benjamin

Turbulence

Budapest

Spilt Milk

Spilt Milk

CHICO BUARQUE

Translated by
Alison Entrekin

Atlantic Books
London

First published in Brazil as *Leite Derramado* in 2009 by Companhia das Letras.

First published in Great Britain in 2012 by Atlantic Books, an imprint of Atlantic Books Ltd.

Copyright © Chico Buarque, 2009
Translation © Alison Entrekin, 2012

 MINISTÉRIO DA CULTURA
Fundação BIBLIOTECA NACIONAL

Obra publicada com o apoio do Ministério da Cultura do Brasil / Fundação Biblioteca Nacional / Coordenadoria Geral do Livro e da Leitura.
This work is published with the support of the Ministério da Cultura do Brasil / Fundação Biblioteca Nacional / Coordenadoria Geral do Livro e da Leitura.

3 5 7 9 10 8 6 4 2

A CIP catalogue record for this book is available from the British Library.

Hardback ISBN: 978 1 84887 488 6
Ebook ISBN: 978 1 78239 014 5

Designed by Nicky Barneby @ Barneby Ltd
Printed and bound by CPI Group (UK) Ltd, Croydon, CR0 4YY

Atlantic Books
An imprint of Atlantic Books Ltd
Ormond House
26–27 Boswell Street
London
WC1N 3JZ
www.atlantic-books.co.uk

Spilt Milk

1

When I get out of here, we'll get married on the farm where I spent my happy childhood, over at the foot of the mountains. You'll wear my mother's dress and veil, and I'm not saying this because I'm feeling sentimental, it's not the morphine speaking. You'll have my family's lace, crystal, silver, jewels and name at your disposal. You'll give orders to the servants, ride my late wife's horse. And if there's still no electricity on the farm, I'll have a generator installed so you can watch TV. There'll also be air conditioning in every room of the farmhouse, because it's very hot on the coastal flats these days. I don't know if it's always been so, if my ancestors sweated under all those clothes. My wife sweated a lot, but she was of a new generation and didn't have my mother's austerity. My wife liked the sun and always came back glowing from afternoons on the sands of Copacabana. But our chalet there has been knocked down, and in any case I wouldn't live with you in a house from a previous marriage. We'll live on the farm at the foot of the mountains.

We'll marry in the chapel that was consecrated by the Cardinal Archbishop of Rio de Janeiro in eighteen hundred and something. On the farm you'll look after me and no one else, so that I'll make a complete recovery. And we'll plant trees, and write books, and, God willing, raise children on my grandfather's land. But if you don't like the foot of the mountains, because of the tree toads and the insects, or the distance, or anything else, we could live in Botafogo, in the mansion my father built. It has huge bedrooms, marble bathrooms with bidets, several drawing rooms with Venetian mirrors and statues, monumentally high ceilings and slate roof tiles imported from France. There are palm, avocado and almond trees in the garden, which became a parking lot after the Danish Embassy moved to Brasilia. The Danes bought the mansion from me for a song because of the mess my son-in-law made of things. But if I decide to sell the farm, with its two thousand acres of crops and pastures, divided by a stream whose water is safe to drink, perhaps I could buy back the mansion in Botafogo, restore the mahogany furniture, have my mother's Pleyel piano tuned. I'll have things to tinker with for years on end, and if you wish to continue working, you'll be able to walk to work, as there are plenty of hospitals and private practices nearby. In fact, they built an eighteen-story medical centre on our land, which reminds me, the mansion isn't there anymore. And come to think of it, I think they expropriated the farm at the foot of the mountains in 1947, for the highway. I'm thinking out loud so you can hear me. And

I'm speaking slowly, as if I were writing, so you can transcribe it for me without having to be a stenographer. Are you there? The soap opera, the news and the film are all over: I don't know why they leave the TV on after the broadcast has finished. It must be so the static will drown out my voice and I won't bother the other patients with my rambling. But there are only grown men here, almost all of them rather deaf. If there were elderly ladies nearby I'd be more discreet. For example, I would never mention the little whores hunkering down in hysterics, as my father tossed five-franc coins onto the floor of his suite at the Ritz. There he'd be, concentrating deeply, while the naked cocottes squatted there like frogs, trying to pick the coins off the rug without using their fingers. He would send the winner down to my room with me, and back in Brazil he would assure my mother I was making good progress with the language. At home, as in all good homes, family affairs were dealt with in French when in the presence of servants, though, for Mother, even asking me to pass the salt was a family affair. And even then she spoke in metaphors, because in those days even your average nurse spoke a little French. But the girl's not in the mood for chit-chat today, she's in a sulk. She's going to give me my injection. The sedative doesn't kick in right away any more, and I know the road to sleep is like a corridor full of thoughts. I hear the noises of people, of viscera, a guy with tubes in him making rasping sounds; perhaps he's trying to tell me something. The doctor on duty will hurry in, take my pulse, perhaps

3

say something to me. A priest will arrive to visit the sick; he'll murmur words in Latin, but I don't think they'll be for me. Sirens outside, telephone, footsteps, there's always an expectation that stops me from falling asleep. It's the hand that holds me by my thinning hair. Until I stumble upon a door to a hollow thought, which will suck me down into the depths, where I tend to dream in black and white.

2

I don't know why you don't try to lessen my pain, Miss. Every day you open the blinds brutishly and the sun strikes me in the face. I don't know what you find so amusing about my grimaces; I feel a twinge every time I breathe. Sometimes I inhale deeply and fill my lungs with an unbearable air, just to have a few seconds of comfort as I exhale the pain. But long before my illness and old age, I suppose my life was already quite like this, a niggling little pain jabbing away at me, then suddenly an excruciating jolt. When I lost my wife, it was excruciating. And anything I remember now is going to hurt; memory is a vast wound. But you still won't give me my meds, you bully. I don't even think you're on the nursing staff; I've never seen your face around here before. Of course, it's my daughter standing with her back to the light. Give me a kiss. I was actually going to call you to come keep me company, read me newspapers, Russian novels. This TV stays on all day long and the people here aren't very sociable. Not that I'm complaining: that would be a sign of ingratitude to you and your son. But if the lad's so rich, I don't know why on earth you don't have me admitted to a traditional care home, run by nuns. I would have been able to pay for travel and treatment abroad myself if your husband hadn't ruined me. I could have taken up residence abroad, spent the rest of my days in Paris. If the urge were to take me, I could die in the same bed at the Ritz that I had slept in as a boy. Because in the summer holidays your grandfather, my father, always took me to Europe by steamer. Later, every time I saw one in the distance, on the Argentine route, I'd call your mother and point: there goes the Arlanza! The Cap Polonio! The Lutétia! And I'd wax lyrical about what an ocean liner was like on the inside. Your mother had never seen a ship close up. After we married she rarely left Copacabana. And when I announced that we'd soon have to go to the docks to meet the French engineer, she got all coy. Because you were a newborn, she couldn't just leave the baby and so on, but then she took the tram into town and cut her hair à la garçonne. When the day came, she dressed as she thought appropriate, in an orange satin dress and an even more orange felt turban. I had already suggested she save the finery for the following month, for the Frenchman's departure, when we could board the ship for a drinks reception. But she was so anxious that she was ready before me and stood waiting by the door. She looked like she were on tiptoe in her high-heeled shoes, and she was either blushing a lot or wearing too much rouge. And when I saw your mother in that state I

6

said, you're not going. Why, she asked in a tiny voice, but I didn't give her a reason, I took my hat and left. I didn't even stop to think about where my sudden anger had come from, all I knew was that the blind anger her cheerfulness provoked in me felt orange. And that's enough talking from me, because the pain is only getting worse.

3

No one believes me, but the woman who came to see me is my daughter. She ended up all skew-whiff like that and missing a few screws because of her son. Or grandson; now I'm not sure if the lad's my grandson or great-great-grandson or what. As the future narrows, younger people have to pile up any which way in some corner of my mind. For the past, however, I have an increasingly spacious drawing room where there is more than enough space for my parents, grandparents, distant cousins and friends from university that I'd already forgotten, with each of their drawing rooms full of relatives and in-laws and gatecrashers with their lovers, as well as all of their memories, all the way back to Napoleon's time. For instance, right now I'm looking at you, so loving with me every night, and I'm embarrassed to ask you your name again. On the other hand, I can recall every hair of my grandfather's beard even though I only knew him from an oil painting. And from the little book that must be over there on the dresser, or upstairs on my mother's bedside table; ask the housemaid. It's a small book with a sequence of almost identical photos, which, when you flick through them, give the illusion of movement, like in the cinema. They show my grandfather walking in London, and when I was a child I liked to flick through them backwards, to make the old boy walk in reverse. It's of these old-fashioned people that I dream, when you tuck me in. If I had my way I would dream of you in Technicolor, but my dreams are like silent films, and the actors died a long time ago. The other day I went to fetch my parents from the playground, because in my dream they were my children. I went to call them with the news that my newborn grandfather was going to be circumcised; he'd become a Jew, just like that. From Botafogo, my dream cut to the farm at the foot of the mountains, where we found my grandfather with a white beard and whiskers, walking in his coat-tails past the British Parliament. He was going at a fast, hard pace, as if he had mechanical legs, thirty feet forward, thirty feet backward, just like in the little book. My grandfather was a prominent figure under the Empire, a Grand Master and a radical abolitionist. He wanted to send all Brazil's blacks back to Africa, but it didn't work out that way. His own slaves, after they had been freed, chose to remain living on his properties. He owned cacao plantations in Bahia, coffee plantations in São Paulo, made a fortune, died in exile and is buried in the family cemetery on the farm at the foot of the mountains, with a chapel blessed by the Cardinal Archbishop of Rio de Janeiro. His closest freed slave, Balbino, faithful as a dog, sat on his grave forever. If you call a taxi, I can show you the farm, the chapel and the mausoleum.

4

Before you show anyone what I'm dictating to you, do me a favour and have a grammarian look over the text so your spelling mistakes won't be imputed to me. And don't forget that my surname is Assumpção, and not Assunção, as it is usually written, as it is probably even written on my chart there. Assunção, the more pedestrian version, was the surname that the slave Balbino adopted, as if asking permission to come into the family barefoot. Interestingly, his son, also Balbino, was my father's stableman. And his son, Balbino Assunção III, a rather chubby black boy, was my childhood friend. He taught me to fly kites, to make traps for hunting birds and the way he used to juggle an orange with his feet fascinated me back when most people hadn't even heard of football. But after I started high school, my trips to the farm grew more infrequent, he grew up without schooling and our affinities dwindled. I would only see him during the July holidays, when from time to time I'd ask him the odd favour, more to make him feel good, as it was his nature to be solicitous. Sometimes I would also ask him to be there on standby, because the farm's calm bored me; in those days we were fast and time dawdled. Hence our endless impatience, and I love watching your young girl's eyes roaming the ward: me, the clock, the TV, your mobile phone, me, the quadriplegic's bed, the drip, the catheter, the old guy with Alzheimer's, your mobile phone, the TV, me, the clock again, and it hasn't even been a minute. I also relish it when you forget your eyes on mine, while you think about the leading man in the soap opera, the messages on your mobile phone, your late period. You look at me just as I used to look at a toad on the farm, hours and hours unmoving, staring at the old toad, so as to let my thoughts wander. At one point, for instance, I got it into my head that I needed to take Balbino up the arse. I was seventeen, maybe eighteen, and I had definitely already been with women, including French ones. So I had no need for it, but right out of the blue I decided I was going to have Balbino. So I'd ask him to go pick a mango, but it had to be a very specific mango, at the top of the tree, one that wasn't even ripe. Balbino would quickly obey, and his long strides from branch to branch began to arouse me for real. No sooner had he reached the particular mango than I would shout a counter order, not that one, the one over there, right at the end. I started to develop a taste for it and not a day went by that I didn't order Balbino to climb the mango trees any number of times. And I began to suspect that the way he was moving about up there wasn't so innocent either, and he had a

14

kind of feminine way of crouching down with his knees together to pick up the mangos that I dropped on the ground. It was clear to me that Balbino wanted me to take him up the arse. I just lacked the courage to make the final move, and went so far as to rehearse some spiel about feudal tradition, droit de seigneur, deliberations so far over his head that he'd give himself to me without a fuss. But as it turned out, fortunately, around this time I met Matilde and got all that nonsense out of my head. I assure you, though, that this association with Balbino left me an adult without prejudice against colour. In that I did not take after my father, who only appreciated blondes and redheads, preferably with freckles. Nor after my mother, who, when she became aware that I had a crush on Matilde, asked me straight off if by any chance the girl had a body odour. Just because Matilde's skin was almost cinnamon. She was the darkest of the Marian congregants that sang at my father's memorial service. I had already glimpsed her on a few occasions, leaving eleven o'clock Mass there at the Church of the Candelária. To be honest, I'd never been able to get a proper look at her because she wouldn't hold still, talking, twirling and disappearing among her friends, her black curls bouncing. She would leave the church as one would the Pathé Cinema, where they showed American serials at the time. But now, just as the organ played the introduction to the offertory, I accidentally let my gaze come to rest on her, glanced away, looked back again and couldn't take my eyes off her after that. Because when she wasn't moving, with her hair up in a bun like that, she was herself even more intensely, with her swaying hidden from sight, her interior agitation, her inward gestures and laughter, forever, oh. Then, I don't know why, in the middle of the church I felt a great urge to know her warmth. I imagined embracing her by surprise, so that she would pulse and writhe against my chest, like smothering in my hands the little bird I'd caught as a boy. There I was, having these profane fantasies, when my mother took my by the arm to take Communion. I hesitated, holding back a little, not feeling worthy of the sacrament, but refusing it in front of everyone would have been discourteous. Feeling a certain fear of hell, I finally went up to kneel at the altar and closed my eyes to receive Holy Communion. When I opened them again, Matilde was facing me, smiling, sitting at the organ that was no longer an organ, but my mother's grand piano. Her hair was wet against her naked back, but now I think I am dreaming already.

5

It's always the way, you people drag me out of bed, trans-
fer me to a stretcher; no one wants to hear of my in-
conveniences. I'm barely awake, no one has brushed
my teeth, my face is still crumpled and unshaven, and
with this wretched appearance you parade me under
the cold light of the corridor, which is a true purgatory,
the maimed strewn about the floor, not to mention the
loafers who come to gawk at misfortune. That's why I
pull the sheet over my once handsome face, which you
quickly expose again so it won't look as if I'm dead,
because it gives a bad impression or perhaps it's demean-
ing for stretcher-bearers to be transporting dead bodies.
Then there's the lift, where everyone stares unceremoni-
ously at my face, instead of looking at the floor, the
ceiling, the floor indicator, because, after all, why not look
at a piece of dirt? Upstairs is another corridor full of zig-
zags and wailing and howling, and finally the old CAT-
scan room, and I don't know who benefits from all this
trouble. I've already had goodness knows how many

X-rays, you've turned me inside out, and in the end you don't say anything; I haven't been shown even a single lung X-ray. Speaking of which, I would love to take a look at my private photos: you, Doctor, you look well bred, if you don't mind, please nip over to my house. Ask my mother to show you the baroque jacaranda desk, whose middle drawer is overflowing with photographs. Look carefully and bring me a photo the size of a postcard, with January 1929 handwritten on the back, showing a small crowd at the quayside with a three-funnel liner in the background. Of the crowd one can only see the backs of their clothes and the tops of their hats, because everyone is facing the Lutétia in the bay. But don't forget also to bring me the magnifying glass, which is always in the smallest drawer, and I'll show you something. If you look carefully, you can see in the photo a single face, of a single man facing the lens, and I assure you that the man in the black suit and bowler hat is me. There's no point in getting a more powerful magnifying glass, because my physiognomy becomes deformed when overly enlarged, you can't see mouth or nose or eyes; it would look like a rubber mask with a dark moustache. And even if the image were sharp, my elegant facial features, when I wasn't yet twenty-two, might strike you as less true to life than a rubber mask. But there I was, and I remember well the people all spellbound by the theatrical appearance of the Lutétia, as she suddenly emerged from the dense fog. At that moment I looked behind me and saw a photographer with his equipment standing some twenty metres away. It wasn't anything new; for some time now such dilettantes and professional photographers could be found everywhere, taking snapshots for posterity's sake, as they used to say. So I presumed, not without vanity, that when the snapshot was developed, I'd be the only one recorded for posterity looking face-on. And after many, many years, after the barrage of time, even then, in some way mine would be a face that survived, because instinct told me to look at the camera at that instant. To accompany this image, I bought another, similar, photograph at a second-hand bookshop, the same size, taken a few hours after the first, from the same angle and with the same lens, obviously by the same photographer. By then the Lutétia had already berthed, and the passengers are walking across the quay, surrounded by friends and family, towards the customs warehouse. I'm down there on the left, next to a taller fellow in a grey or beige suit, with a straw hat slightly crooked on his head. I'm facing the camera again, but this time annoyed at looking almost like a lackey, carrying someone else's overcoat and leather briefcase. The name of the monsieur beside me was Dubosc, and if photographs weren't silent, a very deep voice would be heard rising above all the others, enquiring after the French delegation. He probably still hadn't recognized me at that point because, after dumping his overcoat and briefcase on me, he looked over my head and wouldn't stop saying, l'ambassadeur? l'ambassadeur? It had already been arranged that the ambassador would welcome him with a gala on the Saturday night, with the diplomatic corps, authorities and illustrious members of local society all present, but Dubosc wasn't satisfied. In good French I told him I was enchanted to see him again, after our unforgettable rendezvous in Paris in the company of my late father, Senator Assumpção. But not even the mention of my father had any effect, he insisted on asking after the consul, the military attaché, and protested in a loud voice about the time it was taking to clear his baggage. It's a known fact that some people don't travel well, just as certain wines are upset in transport, which is why I thought it wise to take him to the Palace Hotel in silence, leaving him to his own devices until the following day to recover. I was also keen to get home, where perhaps my wife would thank me for having spared her a tiresome journey. And in the foyer the man already hated the Palace, which, naturally, couldn't compare to the Paris Ritz, but it was the best hotel on Avenida Central, a street that also bored him on account of its European airs. This Dubosc, I'll tell you what, I don't know what became of him, but if he was around forty at the time, by my calculations he died more than twenty years ago. I hope he died in peace among loved ones, of some sudden collapse, so he wouldn't have been in pain his whole life as I have, as my bones and bedsores pain me now as I'm returned to the stretcher. I can just imagine how, in my shoes, he would have blasphemed about the icy temperature in this room and the muggy heat outside. I truly hope he never entered stinking lifts, saw cockroaches like those ones crawling up the walls, tasted the slops of a hospital

20

like this one, or continued to repeat merde alors until the hour of his death. Because everything really is a crock of shit, but then it gets a little better, when at night my girlfriend visits.

6

When I get out of here, we'll start our new life in an old city, where everyone greets everyone else and no one knows us. I'll teach you to speak properly, to use the different types of cutlery and wine glass, I'll carefully choose your wardrobe and serious books for you to read. I sense you have potential because you're hardworking, you have gentle hands and you don't make faces even when you bathe me, in short, you seem like a worthy young lady despite your humble origins. My other wife had a strict upbringing, but even so Mother never understood why I'd chosen her exactly, when there were so many girls from distinguished families to choose from. My mother was from another century, on one occasion she actually asked me if Matilde had body odour. Just because Matilde's skin was almost cinnamon in colour. She was the darkest of her seven sisters, daughters of a federal deputy of the same political party as my father. I don't know if I ever told you that I'd already seen Matilde in passing, in the entrance to the Church of the

Candelária. But I hadn't been able to study her as I did that day, when my eyes settled on her in the pause before the offertory. She was in the choir singing the Requiem, and her Marian habit didn't sit right on her; it seemed to surround her without touching her skin. A garment as rigid as armour, truly alien to her body, and a naked body under it could have danced without being noticed. It was my father's memorial service, but I was unable to free myself of Matilde. I sought to divine her most intimate movements and her far distant thoughts. I registered her blush from afar, her darting eyes, her demure smile as she sang: libera animas omnium fidelium defunctorum de poenis inferni. And it was like an electric shock when Mother touched my elbow, summoning me to Communion. But no sooner had I risen to my feet than I threw myself back into the pew to prevent a scandal. Under no circumstances could I be seen standing, much less beside my mother, in that indecent state. So, covering my face with my hands, passing off my shame as mourning, I tried to think of sad things while Mother consoled me. When I had managed to diminish the inconvenience, I accompanied Mother to the high altar, head down, and took Communion knowing I was committing a sacrilege for which I would soon be punished. And with the wafer still whole on my tongue, almost unintentionally I half-opened my eyes in the direction of the choir, which had dispersed. Full of remorse, I watched the end of the ceremony and then stationed myself alongside my mother to receive the endless queue of sympathies. I accepted formal condolences, emotional outbursts from strangers, sticky hands and foul-smelling breath, without any great hope of Matilde. Until I spotted her beside her parents, then briefly among her sisters, then in the group of Marian congregants. I saw how she approached not in a straight line, but in a spiral, entertaining herself with all and sundry around her, as if she were queuing at an ice cream shop. The closer she came, the more I longed to see her face-to-face, and the more the possibility of losing my composure again tormented me. She arrived, gazed at me with suddenly tear-filled eyes, hugged me and whispered in my ear, courage, Eulálio. Matilde said Eulálio, and confused me. A shiver ran through me as I felt her warm breath in my ear, then a counter-shiver, as I heard a name that almost humiliated me. I didn't want to be Eulálio, only the brothers used to call me that back in high school. I would rather have grown old and been buried with my childhood nicknames, Lalinho, Lalá, Lilico, than been called Eulálio. My Portuguese great-great-great-grandfather's name Eulálio, passing down through great-great-grandfather, great-grandfather, grandfather and father, was for me less of a name than an echo. So I looked her in the eye and said, I don't understand. Matilde repeated, courage, Eulálio, and now, in her slightly hoarse voice, it seemed that my name Eulálio had a texture. She spoke my name as if grazing over it slightly, and when, turning on her heel, she left, I experienced, as I had feared, a new obscene surge. Her six white sisters were already drawing

25

near, directly behind their deputy father, arm-in-arm with their mother, then the Marian congregants, followed by the still long queue, and I had no alternative. I doubled over, clutching my stomach as if in pain, slipped away from my distressed mother and took off through the first door I saw. I crossed the sacristy, startling the priest and his acolytes, and reached a side exit of the church. Seeing people on the pavement, I took off my coat, covered myself and darted down a side street. Soon, on Avenida Beira-Mar, I was able to walk as befitted a gentleman, though without my hat, forgotten on the church pew. And at the end of a long trek I arrived, with my sleeves pushed up, at the mansion in Botafogo, where I saw my mother's old chauffeur leaning against the bonnet of the Ford. I went in through the back door and headed straight upstairs to the bathroom, as I had perspired heavily and was in need of a cold shower. And I had a pressing need to better understand the desire that had so unhinged me; I had never felt anything like it. If that was desire, I can safely say that before Matilde I had been chaste. Perhaps, inadvertently, I had taken possession of my father's libido, just as overnight I had inherited ties, cigars, businesses, real estate and the possibility of a career in politics. It was my father who had introduced me to women in Paris; yet, more than the French girls themselves, I had always been intrigued by the way he looked at them. Just as the aroma of the women here didn't intrigue me as much as his smell, permeating the garçonnière he used to make available to me. In the shower I now looked at myself almost with fear, imagining in my body all of my father's strength and insatiability. Looking down at myself, I had the feeling that my potential for desire was equal to his for every female in the world, but concentrated on just one woman.

7

Good morning, my pretty, but surely there's a less omin-
ous way to wake up than with a daughter snivelling at
one's bedside. And it looks as if you've yet again come
without my cigarettes, much less my cigars. I know smoking isn't allowed in here, but where there's a will there's
a way, and it's not as if I'm asking you to smuggle cocaine
into the hospital. I'm going to tell you the story of how,
one fine day in Paris, your grandfather decided to take
me to a ski resort. Father was a man of many interests,
but until then I hadn't been aware of his sporting side. At
the age of seventeen, he said, it was high time that I
experienced snow, so we took the long train journey to
Crans-Montana, in the Swiss Alps. We checked into the
hotel at night, kitted out with boots and gloves and
woollen beanies, pairs of skis and poles, the works. And I
was about to go to bed when Father called me into his
room, sat down on a chaise longue and opened up an
ebony case. But what's that, Father? Why, it's snow, he
said, looking very serious; Father made a point of always

being serious, regardless of the circumstances. Using a tiny spatula he separated the whitest of white powder into four lines, then passed me a silver straw. And it wasn't that rubbish that any idiot can get hold of; it was pure cocaine, available only to those who could afford it. It didn't leave you with a bitter taste in your mouth or make you lose your appetite, or your hard-on, as he then had the whores sent up. Sometimes I feel sorry for my mother, because Father didn't give her a moment's rest even after he was dead. Your grandmother had to receive the police commissioner into her home and put up with insolent questions, as there was a rumour going round that a cuckold had had my father killed. It was because he'd been machine-gunned down as he entered his garçonnière, but Mother only read O Paiz, whose articles attributed the crime to the opposition. I have to admit, it was not as if tragedy didn't suit Mother; wearing black complimented her nature. Just as all colours seem loud on you and your skin won't tan. I can now admit that I felt sorry for you as a young woman, getting your make-up all wrong. You never convinced me in your glory days, smooching with your boyfriend in a Bentley convertible. You were unrecognisable dressed as a bride, tipsy at the Jockey Club reception; you looked beside yourself with happiness as you waved to me from the deck of the Conte Grande, in dark sunglasses and red gloves. You returned from your honeymoon in high excitement, full of your audience with Pius XII in the Vatican. And I forced myself to share your euphoria, such that I even congratulated you when you showed me your passport, where a Palumba had been added to the surname Assumpção. I admit, I was also amused by Amerigo Palumba, especially when I saw the little shield on his lapel, bearing the crown of the Italian Monarchist Party. The silk handkerchief, the diamond-encrusted buttons, the pearl in the tie; the style wasn't without its charm when you consider that old Palumba Senior had gotten rich gutting pigs in São Paulo. I don't know if the son was ashamed of the sausages, but he must have thanked his lucky stars during the war, when bands of antifascists set fire to their cold storage plants. After the war he came to the capital, began to invest in the stock market, used slang terms to refer to money, and when he took you as a newly-wed to live in a palace in the sky in Flamengo, he tried to impress, telling me how much rent he was paying. And you remained strangely happy, occupied with the decoration of the palace à la Second Empire. You went to the races at the Hipódromo, to the pool at the Copacabana Palace Hotel, and came close to reminding me of your mother when you danced the tango. Until Amerigo Palumba up and vanished on me. The following month, evicted from the palace for insolvency, you returned to normal and, a little stooped, looked at me as if to say, see? The bills poured in, instalments on the convertible, the cruise company, the antique shop, policies, mortgages and promissory notes started to arrive from every direction, and you'd say, didn't I tell you? Of Amerigo Palumba I received dubious news. I don't know if he sank my money into aristocratic titles; some even say he became an intimate of the dethroned king of Italy. He was seen losing large sums of money at the casino in Estoril, to the delight of some old dukes, because making money at roulette was so nouveau riche. It was as the old phrase goes: wealthy father, titled son, poor grandson. It just so happened that the poor grandson was in your belly, Eulálio d'Assumpção Palumba, the strapping young boy we brought up, who grew to be rebellious and with good reason. He returned to the straight and narrow as an adult, but you must remember when he took it into his head to become a communist. Imagine what your grandmother would have said: her granddaughter married to an immigrant's son and her great-grandson a communist of Chinese sympathies. That boy of yours knocked up another communist, who had a son in prison and in prison passed away. You say he died at the hands of the police, and I do have a vague recollection of such a thing. But an old man's memory can't be trusted, and now I'm sure I saw the boy just the other day, alive and kicking. He even gave me a box of cigars, but wait, my mistake, the one who died was another Eulálio, one that looked like a thinner Amerigo Palumba. The thin Eulálio is the one who became a communist, because he was born in prison and they say he was weaned too soon. As a result, he smoked marijuana, hit his teachers, and was expelled from all his schools. But even though he was semi-illiterate and a pyromaniac, he found work and prospered; the other day he gave me a box of cigars. He visited me at my place with a girlfriend with her midriff bare and an earring in her bellybutton. I wouldn't have minded that one as a daughter-in-law, but the one who gave birth in prison was another. I will never forget the day they called me to collect the baby from the army hospital. The colonel was polite, said he knew me from elsewhere. I was even somewhat moved when I saw the little guy, practically an orphan, because Amerigo Palumba was far away and you were in prison, locked away and incommunicado. But wait a second, that's not possible because you left the hospital with me, with the baby in your arms. All I know is that Eulálio d'Assumpção Palumba Junior was baptized and raised by us. He's the one who now takes you for rides in his car and gives me Cuban cigars. He came over here to my place the other day with a girlfriend with a pin in her bellybutton, who didn't seem like a communist at all. Nor does the lad strike me as the kind who would distribute pamphlets against the dictatorship. You must be confusing him with someone else, that darker-skinned Eulálio, the skirt-chaser, who was involved with a Japanese girl and got his cousin pregnant. But that one, if I'm not mistaken, was the son of the strapping young Eulálio and the belly-button girl; sometimes my mind gets a bit confused. It's all a tremendous jumble, my dear, aren't you even going to give me a kiss? It's not pleasant being abandoned like this, talking at the ceiling.

8

Memory is truly a pandemonium, but it's all in there: after rummaging around a little the owner can find all manner of things. What isn't right is for someone from the outside to meddle with it, like the maid who moves one's papers to dust the office. Or the daughter who wants to arrange my memory in her own order, chronological, alphabetical, or by subject. Some time back I found a certain colonel in a dark corridor of the army hospital. He said he'd last seen me when he was still a third sergeant, but his face in the half-light didn't ring any bells. Nor did mine for him, I'm sure, since he'd recognized me by my name. But the recollection wasn't mutual, and in such cases, so as not to offend, one usually says, ah, yes, of course, how are you, and that's that. Because scouring one's memory all the time is tiresome, but he really believed I was making an effort to remember him, and wanted to help. And he only confused me further when he said, in French, that forty years fly by, and I wasn't sure if he was quoting some poet. I was about to excuse myself when he mentioned the artillery tests at Marambaia and I don't know why he hadn't done so sooner: it all came to me in a flash. Rifling through files of names and faces would have been useless, because my memory had preserved the sergeant in the landscape. It was a sunny day and, from the top of the dune, I was gazing at the narrowest stretch of a spit of land, a line of the whitest sand, which the ocean hadn't swallowed up, on some whim, or out of pity, maternal zeal or sadism. The waves foamed simultaneously to the right and left of the spit, like a beach looking in a mirror. At the foot of my dune was the sergeant, with a group of young soldiers, all wearing olive-green trousers, without jackets, their sodden T-shirts clinging to their bodies. He was helping position a cannon in the sand, as instructed by the French engineer. He stood out from the others as he appeared to have some knowledge of the language and was ever ready to translate the instructions for his colleagues, which left me free to let my mind roam. The heavy work had the young men panting, but it was Dubosc, sitting on a box of ammunition, who most seemed to be suffering from the heat. And it turned out that all the effort was in vain, because when the battery was finally in position and ready to fire, we received news that the minister of war had cancelled his visit to the demonstration. The sergeant translated the courier's message, but it was to me that Dubosc turned. And I must say, the Frenchman's bad humour was prophetic, because sooner or later his peeves always proved him right. It was my job to absorb his outbursts of rage; for two hours in the car to the Palace Hotel I served as his punch bag. Two-faced, perfidious, incompetent, indolent, tardy, and even a bad driver. I listened to a great many insults in silence, because I knew they weren't actually addressed to me, but to my fellow countrymen in general. Dubosc went overboard from time to time: he was a highly strung engineer. He'd barely set foot in the country and wanted to find every door open, or else blow them open with dynamite. I, on the other hand, knew that the doors were just pulled to; my father had been through them before. Being young and inexperienced, as by appearance the Frenchman judged me to be, the next day I might have found myself lost in a labyrinth with seven hundred doors. But I had no doubt that, for me, the right door would open on its own. Behind it, precisely the person I was looking for would call me by name. And they'd promptly announce me to the influential person, who'd come down the stairs to fetch me. And they'd open up their chambers, where there'd be several phone calls waiting for me. And over the phone, powerful people would whisper the words they wanted to hear. And with my eyes closed, along the way I'd grease the same palms my father had greased. And for three times the price that had been agreed, they'd buy the cannons, the howitzers, the rifles, the grenades and all the ammunition the Company had to sell. My name is Eulálio d'Assumpção and for no other reason did Le Creusot & Cie. appoint me its representative in this country. And while I saw to it that things were taken care of, it was probably a good thing that Dubosc went on boat trips to unwind or travelled up to the mountains to hunt capybara, always with his acquaintances from the French colony. But he had no qualms about calling me late at night, for lack of a better companion, to escort him to a restaurant or a dance hall. When he was off the job he revealed a different temperament, bragging about his progress in tango, foxtrot, Charleston and maxixe classes; the latest novelty was the samba. And once, at the Assirius Cabaret, after dancing with some young ladies from another table, he ordered another lime cocktail and asked me why I never brought my wife, whom everyone said was so charming. I don't know where he got that from; no one from his circle knew Matilde. He also said that on the phone my wife had a warm voice and spoke excellent French. That, I'm sure, he said to flatter me, and it made me laugh because Matilde's French was all but broken. I had actually considered taking her to the reception at the embassy, and she'd painted her nails and picked out an orange dress for the occasion. But I'd decided it wasn't worth it; Matilde would have felt out of place in such circles. She wasn't interested in politics; in business, even less. She loved westerns, but couldn't sustain a conversation about literature. She knew little about the sciences, geography and history, though she had studied at the Sacré Coeur. At sixteen, when she dropped out to marry me, she still hadn't completed high school. She had studied piano, like all girls of her position in life, but she didn't shine at that either. We were still courting the day she sat at my mother's Pleyel and I prepared to hear a piece by Mozart, the composer whose work she had sung, or pretended to sing, at my father's memorial service. But instead she banged out a foot-stomper called Voodoo Ditty; goodness only knows where she had learned that. And Mother came hurrying down the stairs to see what on earth was going on. The next day she asked me if Matilde's parents had given her permission to be alone with me at our place every day after class. Little did she know that, by night, I secretly watched the back garden from my window, waiting for Matilde to steal onto the lawn on tiptoe, between the almond trees and the servants' quarters. I would race downstairs and open the kitchen door, and Matilde would barely cross the threshold. She would lean against the kitchen wall, her breathing short, and open her black eyes wide. In silence we'd stare at one another for five, ten minutes, Matilde with her hands at hip level, clutching, twisting her own skirt. And she would slowly blush until she was a deep red, as if, in ten minutes, an afternoon of sun had passed across her face. A palm's distance away from her, I was the biggest man in the world: I was the sun. I'd see her lips part slightly, and above them tiny beads of sweat would appear, as her eyelids slowly relaxed. Finally I would throw myself against her body, pressing her against the kitchen wall, with no skin contact and no hands or legs moving forward, according to some unspoken agreement. I'd crush her with my torso almost, until she said, I'm coming, Eulálio, and her

39

whole body would shudder, causing mine to shudder with it. An unsettled feeling would follow, then meandering thoughts, the neighbour's dog, the cold beer in the Frigidaire, the warmth moving down my thighs, the dog, my sticky trousers and underpants, the Frigidaire that my father had sent for from the United States, the laundress showing Mother my clothes, the beer in the Frigidaire that Father never got to see. When I came to my senses, I would be pressed against the tiled wall, because Matilde always slipped away. And every time I would go to inspect the drawing rooms, bedrooms, bathrooms, the basement and the attic, pretending that I believed that she had accidentally fled into the house. A long time later, after she had left my life, I maintained the fanciful habit of looking for her like that, every night, in the chalet in Copacabana. And I left all the doors open for her until the end, but I shouldn't be talking so much about my wife to you. Here you come with the syringe; sleep will do me good, take my arm.

9

When I die, my chalet will fall with me, to make way for another apartment building. It will have been the last house in Copacabana, which, by that time, will be just like the island of Manhattan, bristling with skyscrapers. But before that, Copacabana will be like Chicago, with policemen and gangsters exchanging gunfire in the streets, though I'll sleep with my doors open nevertheless. I don't mind if degenerates wander through my house, and beggars and cripples and lepers and junkies and nutcases, as long as they let me sleep in. Because every day it's the same thing: I wake up with the sun on my face, the TV blaring, and I understand now that I'm not in Copacabana and the chalet's been gone for more than half a century. I'm in this pestilent hospital, no offence intended to those present. I don't know who you people are, I don't know your names, I can barely turn my head to see what you look like. I hear your voices, and I can tell that you're commoners, not in any way particularly remarkable, but my lineage doesn't

make me better than anyone else. Here I enjoy no priv-
ileges. I howl with pain but they don't give me my
opiates; we all sleep in creaking beds. It would even be
comical if, sitting here in shitty nappies, I told you that I
was well born. No one will care if, for example, my great-
great-grandfather disembarked in Brazil with the
Portuguese court. It would be useless to brag that he was
a confidant of Queen Maria the Mad if no one here
has any idea who she was. Today I belong to the dregs of
society, just like you, and before I was admitted, I lived
with my daughter in a borrowed one-room hut at the
end of the earth. I can barely afford cigarettes, nor do I
have the right clothes to leave the house. The only reason
I remember the last time I went out was because of a
disagreement with a taxi driver. He didn't want to wait
for even half an hour for me in front of Cemitério São
João Batista, and because he was addressing me rudely, I
lost my head and raised my voice, listen here, mister, I'm
the great-grandson of the Baron dos Arcos. So he told me
to go fuck myself and the baron too, and I can hardly
blame him. It was very hot in the car, he was a sweaty
mulatto, and I was putting on airs and graces. I acted like
a snob, which, as you must know, means an individual
lacking in nobility. Many of you, if not everyone here,
are descended from slaves, which is why I am proud to
say that my grandfather was a great benefactor of the
Negro race. I'll have you know he visited Africa in eighteen hundred and something, dreaming of founding a
new nation for your ancestors. He travelled on a cargo

ship to Luanda, passed through Nigeria and Dahomey, and finally, on the Gold Coast, he discovered a community of old freedmen from Bahia, named Tabom because they still used the Portuguese expression tá bom. And they repeated it to my grandfather, tá bom, okay, as if to confirm that the Gold Coast was an auspicious land for such an undertaking. And after establishing a partnership with the English colonists, my grandfather launched a campaign in Brazil to found Nova Liberia. Grandpa was a true visionary; he designed the country's flag himself, multi-coloured stripes with a gold triangle in the centre and an eye inside the triangle. He commissioned the great composer Carlos Gomes to write the national anthem, while British architects planned the future capital, Petróvia. He won the support of the Church, the Freemasons, the press, bankers, farmers and the emperor himself, everyone thought it was right that the children of Africa might return to their roots instead of wandering around Brazil in abject poverty and ignorance. But you people aren't interested in any of this, and you even turn up the TV over my already shaky voice. I was going to say that my grandfather was often invited to dinner by Pedro II of Brazil, that he exchanged letters with Queen Victoria, but I'm forced instead to watch these bizarre dancers with their dyed-blonde hair. And without so much as an excuse me, the stretcher-bearers drag me off again for a CAT scan. It's always the same; off they charge with my stretcher. These hairpin bends and ramps are more like the racing circuit; any day now I'm going to be in a fatal accident. All this for yet another routine exam, and maybe you, Doctor, being a man of good standing, can get me transferred to a traditional care home, run by nuns. Just between you and me, I've been feeling quite agitated lately; I'm sure they're switching my medications. I wouldn't be surprised if they put arsenic in my food, and if it comes to the worst, mark my words, the newspapers will undertake to make it public. And they'll dredge up the murder of my father, an important politician, as well as a learned, handsome man. You should know, sir, that my father was one of the first republicans, a friend of presidents. His brutal death even made headlines in Europe, where he enjoyed great prestige and acted as a coffee broker. He traded with arms dealers in France, had powerful friends in Paris, and at the turn of the century, when he was still very young, did business with English entrepreneurs. A practical soul, he went into partnership with the English to build the harbour in Manaus, but didn't join the African adventures of his father, another victim of jealousy and slander. I'll have you know that my grandfather was born into money; he wouldn't have sullied his name embezzling public funds. But with the end of the Empire, he had to seek asylum in London, where he died a bitter man. Take it easy with the stretcher, you lot, careful as you lie me back in bed, and get me silk-cotton pillows for my back and bottom, because my bedsores and my joints hurt. If I'm poisoned to death tomorrow, everyone here will see me on the TV that no one ever turns off. The health department will shut this pigsty down, and I'll be back to haunt you, and you'll all sleep in the street.

10

If it were up to me, I wouldn't celebrate any birthday, but the boy turned up at my place without warning. He showed me off to his girlfriend with her bare midriff. It was Grandpa this, Grandpa that, and my daughter was the only one who wasn't amused. Although he was having fun at my expense, I know the boy was proud of my one hundred years; everyone is proud of long-lived relatives. I'd like to have met my great-great-grandfather too. I wish my father had stuck around a bit longer, and, above all, I wish Matilde had survived me and not the other way around. I don't know if there is such a thing as destiny, if someone spins it, rolls it, cuts it. In a spinner's fingers, the thread of Matilde's life would probably have been of better fibre than mine, and longer. But often a life will stop halfway, not because the thread is short, but because it is tortuous. I can't even begin to imagine the suffering of Matilde's life after she left me. I know mine has become unbearably long, like a fraying thread. Without Matilde, I wandered about crying out loud, perhaps like those freed slaves people talk about. It was as if I tore a little with each step, because my skin had snagged on hers. One day Mother called me over to talk, I think she was a little disappointed to discover that someone was unhappier than she. She refrained from mentioning Matilde's name, as she knew the wound still stung, and offered me a ticket to Europe. With her eyes lowered, she handed me my father's Paris address book, saying, I hope you have a good time, Eulálio. I don't know if her calling me Eulálio was a lapse, since I'd always been Lalinho to her, mainly because it was a way of distinguishing me from her husband. I thanked her, refusing the ticket and address book, but Mother intended to cure me by force and imposed the trip on me like a spoonful of cough syrup in a child's mouth. Because if I didn't, she'd go to Europe herself. She would go and play the heavy with my father's financial agents, who hadn't answered her telegrams. She would wear the trousers, and I'd be a grown man on an allowance. It hadn't even been a month since Le Creusot had let me go, in spite of their trust in me until very recently. So much so that they had even sent me a new shipment of mortars and modern sighting devices to replace the army's already obsolete materiel before it had even been sold. Things were moving a little slower here than expected. Getting customs clearance for bombs and explosives, for example, was something my father used to do with a phone call, or via any customs broker. I, on the other hand, had to turn up early at the bureau, stand elbow-to-elbow with strangers, flash my calling card, get the official's attention: listen here, sir, my name is Eulálio d'Assumpção. I remember the surprise of the fellow who finally saw me. The senator? His son, I answered, and watched him sidle over to his colleagues. From their whispering I understood that my father, an important figure in the Republic, had fallen into disrepute among the people. Assunção, the murderer? Assunção, the cuckold? The political moment was also delicate; ministers hummed and hawed, and we sat out many hours in government antechambers, Dubosc and I. The Frenchman, who had imagined he'd only be here a month, launched projectiles into the Atlantic Ocean over and over for almost a year to impress low-ranking officers, or just to let off steam. I wouldn't be surprised if in his reports to the Company he made comments that were damaging to my professional reputation. And if I were vindictive, I would have taken advantage of my trip to report Dubosc's nocturnal activities in Rio to company headquarters, not to mention his hunting in the mountains and his excursions to Mato Grosso looking for forest-dwelling Indians at his employers' expense. That's what I was musing over on the quarterdeck of the Lutétia as the city disappeared from sight, when the butler came to greet me. I was known from other voyages on that ship, and the staff all offered me their condolences for the senator's passing. Father was admired there for his impeccable French and generous tips, especially on the way out, or en route to civilization, as he used to say. And on the very first night I was invited to dine with the captain,

49

who, in front of the architect Le Corbusier and the singer Josephine Baker, proposed a toast to the memory of my father and remembered that he was quite the ladies' man. Enthused, I told them about his vigorous friend La Comtesse, who practiced the Singapore grip with half-franc coins, but the captain didn't really get it, and the singer struck up a parallel conversation with the architect. On the following nights I was seated at a table with Argentineans, and my status on the Lutétia slowly waned, perhaps because my father's fluent French was beginning to fail me. Or because the cash I was carrying, like everything that came from my mother, was modest. I would sit at the bar after midnight, and the barman would automatically pour me a glass of Krug, the senator's champagne. I'd let the drink go warm in the glass, smoking black cigarettes, and there was always a table of high-spirited Brazilians nearby, talking about livestock, plantations, land, money. Northerners, my father used to say, but those guffawing men outdid him by a mile as far as tips went, handing them out with fanfare. The bar closed at sunrise, and I would go to bed rather seasick. I'd cover the porthole of my cabin in the stern so as not to see the accumulation of ocean that was taking me further and further away from my wife. I wondered if I had become somewhat rooted in the land, which, according to my father, was typical of Northerners. And by the time I disembarked at Bordeaux, where there was no one to greet me, I was convinced I was making my last visit to civilization. In Paris I was received with disbelief and was asked if we didn't get world news in South America. Coffee imports had been embargoed across Europe more than a month earlier, rendering my father's wholesale partners bankrupt. In London, they told me about financial disasters, millions of pounds sterling annihilated overnight as a consequence of the Wall Street Crash. Along with the Assumpção family assets, ill-advisedly invested in the United States stock market. They say bad things never come alone, and it's a good thing; my misfortune would have been even more painful if I hadn't already taken a fall. I was actually grateful to the man for coming straight to the point and the swift conclusion to our meeting. I took an express train to Southampton, and everywhere I went I felt people staring at me with the mistrust aroused by a taciturn foreigner. I would rather they had pointed and laughed at me, as they did in the streets of Rio de Janeiro, where the reasons for my suffering were known. At the last minute I sailed home on a Dutch cargo ship, where I even got a bunk in the prow. As for money, whether I liked it or not, Mother would always be my safety net. Her family was, perhaps, wealthier than Father's. The Montenegros owned half of the state of Minas Gerais in pasture alone. It is true that the family was large, as Mother had some twenty brothers and sisters, but a single dairy farm would be enough to keep me going, even if I lived a hundred years. My little girl would grow up surrounded by the best things money could buy, and my wife would live in greater opulence, if she ever came home.

51

11

I was beginning to think you weren't coming, that it was your day off. The other girl isn't a bad person, but in her hurry she always knocks over my medication, and doesn't take note of the things I say. So, if you go on holiday tomorrow, please let me know before you go. I notice you've been on edge recently; I worry you'll become weary of everything and leave again for good. You can be sure that I'll never ask where you spend your afternoons, nor do I want to know if you go to the cinema with the doctors. When I get out of here, I'm going to take you with me everywhere, I won't be ashamed of you. I won't criticize your dress, your manners, your choice of language, or even your whistling. With time I have learned that jealousy is an emotion to announce with an open heart, at the very moment of its origin. Because at its birth, it is a truly courteous sentiment and should be offered to a lady like a rose. Otherwise, the next moment it closes up like a cabbage and inside it all evil ferments. Jealousy is, then, the most introverted kind of envy and, seething with rage, blames others for its ugliness. Knowing itself to be despicable, it goes by many other names: as an example, I offer my poor grandmother, who knew her jealousy as rheumatism. They say she howled at the pain in her joints, there on the farm at the foot of the mountains, every time my grandfather went chasing slave women. But she claimed to be indifferent to the wanderings of her husband, who'd always had this vice. The son of a slave-trading baron, he had sported with the Negresses on his father's properties from the moment he was out of nappies. My grandmother wouldn't let it go, swearing her husband had fathered his faithful servant Balbino's children. She would say these things with resignation in her soul, but riddled with so much physical pain that my grandfather sent for rheumatologists from all over Europe. In the end he brought out a Swiss contractor, who built a chalet on the distant sands of Copacabana. And Grandpa isolated her there to ease her suffering with therapeutic bathing. I, on the other hand, married and went to live with Matilde in the old chalet with the intention of spending my whole life with her. I only left to go to work, which didn't require much of me at first. All I had to do was put on one of my father's English ties and go where he had gone, as Mother wished me to, until I got into my stride. In the Senate I was always well received, I would take coffee in various offices, circulate along the corridors, hang around smoking; not infrequently I'd be invited to lunch with politicians at La Rôtisserie. If not, I'd eat alone at a canteen, then stop by the Le Creusot office, taking a bonbon for the secretary, ask after a cablegram and sit in the chair my father had left vacant. With my feet on the desk, I'd smoke and stare at the phone, ready to take over Father's role in an instant. Every now and then I'd pay a visit to the O Paiz newsroom, have a coffee, light a cigar, duck into the bank, and I'd be home before four. By the time I got out of the car, I would be longing to hear Matilde's strange records, the phonograph I'd given her for her birthday. If there was no music, I'd go down to the beach to drag her back home, and the maid knew it was time to head out to the grocer's, anticipating a racket. We would go at it in the kitchen, the living room, on the stairs, for hours and hours in the shower; we could spend an entire weekend in bed. Sometimes we would go for a drive on Sundays, but we hardly spent any time at Mother's mansion, as Matilde didn't care to. She preferred to visit the farm because she loved to ride, and when I trotted behind her I would become perturbed, almost feeling desire for the horse. And I'll never forget our agitation when she had premature contractions while galloping in the middle of nowhere. Fortunately, we made it home in time to call the obstetrician and nurses and Maria Eulália was born healthy, a little on the small side because she was two months premature. I also remember how, without saying a word, Matilde became annoyed with my mother, who only gave the baby blue boy's clothes. Mother's excuse was that she had sent them to be embroidered well in advance, because the Assumpção family only had male offspring. And she told me that they only ever had one child; it was a family curse. Before me she'd lost five herself, and five times had narrowly escaped dying of eclampsia. But Matilde had always been full of health, and the following week she was back on the beach in a swimsuit, her body better than ever. Out of spite, she never took our daughter to see her grandmother; she waited for the girl's grandmother to come and visit, and the few times she did, Matilde showed her little Eulália naked. Nor did Matilde wear the long-sleeved dresses that Mother had given her, which was unfair to the dresses. I suggested a high-necked grey one when we went out to dance because it was a cool night. But she insisted on the strappy orange one. And when I opened the car door for her to get in, I looked at her naked shoulders and thought I'd never seen her so beautiful. I also saw a bit of her tanned thighs when the doorman of the Assirius opened the door for her to get out. Dubosc was waiting for us at the entrance to the hall and bowed low to kiss her hand: Jean-Jacques, enchanté. Our table was near the orchestra, and with his trombone-like voice he asked the waiter for a lime cocktail. It was the only thing he knew how to say in Portuguese, batida de limão, and I asked him to repeat it because Matilde found his accent funny. Dubosc began to praise our fauna, flora and waterfalls, but I'm not sure Matilde understood him. Although she looked at him very attentively, sitting on the edge of her chair, I realized she was dancing the foxtrot from the waist down. And she drummed her fingers on the table

to the beat of the Charleston while I described for her
the ochre cliffs of Roussillon, our friend Dubosc's home-
land, in a loud voice. At that moment the orchestra
started to belt out the song I'd heard so often in the distance, on Matilde's phonograph. Le maxixe! exclaimed
the Frenchman, this Negro rhythm is magnificent! and
he asked us to dance it for him. But I only knew how to
waltz, and answered that he'd be doing me an honour by
asking my wife to dance. In the middle of the floor they
embraced and just stood there, staring at one another.
Suddenly he twirled her around, then moved his left foot
back, while she took a long step forward with her right,
and they froze again, Matilde arching over his body. The
choreography was precise, and I was surprised that my
wife knew the steps. They understood one another perfectly, but I soon distinguished what for him was learned
from what for her was natural. Very tall, the Frenchman
was a stick puppet playing with a rag doll. Perhaps in
contrast, she shone among the dozens of dancers, and I
noticed that the entire cabaret was fascinated by their
exhibition. On close examination, however, the people
there were tastelessly dressed, ornamented and painted,
and I began to feel that in Matilde too, in her shoulder
and hip movements, there was excess. The orchestra
didn't let up, the music was repetitive and the dance
turned out to be vulgar; for the first time it struck me that
the woman I'd married was slightly vulgar. After half
an hour they returned fanning themselves, and sweat
ran down Matilde's chest and into her cleavage. Bravo,

I cried, bravo, and even encouraged them to dance the next tango, but Dubosc said it was already late and that I looked fatigued. He was the one who was fatigued and asked for a lift to his hotel two blocks away. He got out without saying goodbye properly and didn't even kiss Matilde's hand. Maybe he had concluded, over the course of the evening, that she was the kind of woman with whom one danced the maxixe, not the kind whose hand one kissed. And on the way home, Matilde started whistling the tune of the maxixe. It struck me as childish; she had once whistled at a dinner party of my mother's, who had left the table. But this time she must have realized how much it exasperated me, because she stopped and asked what was wrong. Nothing, heartburn, I said, and it wasn't a lie. Cachaça, which was now popular even in fancy places, didn't agree with me. She got out of the car before I could open the door for her and no sooner had we entered the house than she headed for the kitchen; she was always going off to the kitchen. She often took our daughter there and chatted with the servants. Not infrequently she lunched there with the nursemaid. I found myself gripped by an obscure sentiment somewhere between shame and rage for loving a woman who was always in the kitchen. I followed Matilde as she talked to herself, asking, half-crooning, if there was any boldo tea, and I don't know what came over me. I suddenly grabbed her violently from behind and threw her against the wall; she didn't understand and started to moan nasally, her face smashed against the tiles. I clamped her fists to the wall and she struggled, but I controlled her with my knees behind hers. And I squeezed her, pressing hard, almost crushing her with my torso, until Matilde said, I'm coming, Eulálio, and her whole body shuddered, causing mine to shudder with it.

12

This was my last night here, and the last night I made these sheets sticky dreaming of her. As I do every morning, I'll pull off the bedclothes and make a bundle, which I'll throw out the back window for the laundress to catch. But a wet stain will still be visible on the mattress, which I'll turn over as I do every morning, leaving it dry-stains-up. I'll have the feeling that the mattress weighs a little more every day, and I'll imagine the sap of my dreams and solitary acts impregnating its straw stuffing. And I'll think that, if I'd turned my father's body over in the garçonnière, he'd weigh as much as the mattress and give off the same smell. I'll always remember my father face-down on the bloody carpet, and how the senior detective wouldn't let me touch his body. There was no need for him to yell at me, or grab my arm; I just didn't want to leave my father there like that, with his mouth open on the carpet. And I wanted to understand where so many bullets had entered, because it seemed that all of the blood in his body had exited through his mouth, that great ulcer. But you always interrupt me, ma'am, with this business of Sir. I have already told you I'm not a knight. I am the great-grandson of the Baron dos Arcos, and, as you're well aware, I'm a patient of your establishment. I've also told you that the p in Assumpção is silent. Pronounced, it sounds mocking, as if you were insinuating that we are a family of pedants. And since you're holding a pen and paper, it wouldn't hurt you to make some notes to help your employee out. The poor thing makes peanuts working the night shift; she looks after everyone at the same time and has to write my memoirs to boot. When you awoke me, coincidentally, I had just woken up in the Botafogo mansion, and I bet my mother had the mattress burned that very day. The chalet in Copacabana had a double bed, otherwise she would have sent it with the move. Mother reused what she could to furnish the house, and she bought some furniture second hand, because the hasty renovations had already cost her quite a sum. My wedding announcement had caught her off guard, and she even refused me her blessing if I didn't finish my degree or get a job. A law degree was out of the question as I had barely set foot in the university, but I got a job immediately. Matilde's father received me with open arms, assured me that there would always be a place for Senator Eulálio d'Assumpção's son on his staff, and even undertook to expedite my membership of the party. With great swagger, I reported my success to my mother, who lost her composure and asked if I had already forgotten my father's murder. For an instant

I stood there gaping, I couldn't see my future father-in-law holding a pistol, much less his fat wife embroiled in a crime of passion. But my mother was referring to our political opponents, who, as far as she was concerned, had always been behind it. I hadn't been paying much attention to the news and wasn't aware that Matilde's father, whose career had flourished in my father's shadow, had cheerfully swung over to the opposition. Knowing she couldn't compete with Matilde, Mother offered me an allowance of three million réis, plus the refurbishment of the chalet, as long as I rejected the traitor's proposal. I ended up getting four million and the used Ford as a bonus, after pointing out to her that a deputy's adviser earned no less than that. I went to my future father-in-law and thanked him for the opportunity, but told him that my roots in the conservative camp wouldn't allow me to serve a liberal politician. He replied that he respected my convictions, but couldn't entrust his almost pubescent daughter's hand to an individual who couldn't keep his word. That was when Matilde played her trump card, informing her parents that she was pregnant. It wasn't true: Matilde had always insisted on maintaining her virginity until she was married. But for a federal deputy, no matter how liberal, an unwed daughter with a child was an inconvenience. So he ceded his daughter, and his constituents never knew that he disinherited her at the same time. Since no one knew about the wedding either, the ceremony at the mansion was discreet, we didn't have invitations printed and the banns were run in one of those papers that respectable people don't read. Mother requested that the priest come from the Church of the Candelária, and I thought I saw him blush when he saw me standing before him. He delivered the sermon with his head bowed, and he had an even sorrier look about him than he had at my father's memorial service, perhaps troubled by Matilde's informal dress, with its pattern of red flowers. My witnesses were Mother and Auguste, the chauffeur my father had imported from France together with his first Peugeot, before the war. On Matilde's side we improvised with Uncle Badeco, a brother of Mother's who happened to be passing through Rio de Janeiro. And the fourth witness would have been the laundress, but she was replaced at the last minute by Matilde's mother, who made a surprise appearance when the ceremony was already well under way. She was wearing the same hat that she had worn at my father's service, with a dark veil covering her face, and she was the only one to take Communion, along with Mother. After that they became close friends and often took tea and sponge cake together in the mansion, as they shared their griefs. And one day Matilde's fat mother let slip that the girl was not her daughter, but the consequence of an adventure the federal deputy had had up in Bahia. Mother lost no time in calling me over to her place, and made the revelation in my father's library, where serious matters were handled. He must have others, she said, the traitor must have other families up there. And after a sigh she added, Northerners. If you ask me, it was all a fabrication,

Matilde's mother seeking to exempt herself from blame for not having stood up for her daughter when her husband rejected her. I didn't take the matter any further, and I'm sure Matilde would have laughed at it. Just as today I chuckle at my childish outrage when a rumour went around school that I was adopted. It was trivial teasing, which can happen to any child, and even Mother laughed a little when she heard my story. But she must have noticed that it got to me, because a short time later, in a moment of fury, she used it to punish me. On that occasion, my father was presiding over the Senate Agriculture Committee on agrarian matters, and there had been an uprising of religious fanatics in the South. Every night a secretary would call to let Mother know not to wait up, because the senator would be tied up until the following day in continuous session, or in conference at the army headquarters, or behind closed doors with President Venceslau. Mother must have been used to it as my father often spent the night out; all it took was for the country to experience a crisis. But she'd always be on edge, wandering around the house in circles, aimlessly going up and down the stairs, and I'd take the opportunity to wind her up a little more. I would kick the maids, pretend to faint; that day I put my elbows on the table and ate with my mouth open. After reprimanding me twice, three times, Mother sent me to finish lunch in the kitchen. So I goaded her; with my mouth wide open I showed her my mouthful of rice, beans, meat and potato, and I think I actually wanted to be slapped about the face a bit. Just as, from time to time, I think I also missed pulling down my trousers for my father to whip me with his belt. Afterwards, I liked to climb up on to the bathroom stool, sobbing, to see the buckle-marks on my buttocks in the mirror over the sink. And when Mother got up from the head of the table and marched toward me, I got ahead of myself and started crying and pissing myself before the blow. She raised her open hand, but changed her mind at the last minute. Staring at me closely, she said that none of the Montenegros of Minas Gerais had thick lips like mine. I spat the food onto the plate, but the insult has been stuck in my throat all these years. And now I asked her in passing, as we left the library, why she had never told me that Uncle Badeco Montenegro wore an Afro.

13

Eulálio Montenegro d'Assumpção, 16 June 1907, widower. Father, Eulálio Ribas d'Assumpção, like the street behind the metro station. Though for two years he was a tree-lined square in downtown Rio, then the liberals seized power and renamed it after a caudillo from the South. You must have read somewhere, ma'am, that in 1930 the Gauchos invaded the capital, tied their horses to the obelisk and threw our traditions into the rubbish. Some time later, an enlightened mayor resuscitated my father, by giving his name to a tunnel. But along came the military government and deposed Father for the second time, renaming the tunnel after a lieutenant who'd lost his leg. Then, with the advent of democracy, a Green councillor gave my father that dead-end street, goodness knows why. My grandfather is also a side street, over by the docks. And on my mother's side, Rio de Janeiro looks like a family tree; if you don't believe me have an errand boy go buy a map of the city. Those are my personal details, if you want to update my record. The rest is trifle

with which I don't concern myself. In fact, I didn't ask
to be here; the person who had me admitted was my
daughter. Health insurance isn't my department, and if
it hasn't been paid, please speak to Maria Eulália Vidal
d'Assumpção Palumba. For accounting purposes, my ex-
penses are paid by my great-great-grandson, Eulálio
d'Assumpção Palumba III. And if you really must know
how he makes his money, I assure you I haven't the
slightest idea. I'm very grateful to the boy, but to make
millions without any education, he must be a film actor
or worse, you can write that there. But you don't take note
of anything, you shake your head and look at me as if I
were talking nonsense. People don't take the trouble to
listen to old-timers, and that's why so many of them just
sit there gaping, staring into space, in a kind of foreign
land. The one who talks nonsense is my daughter, who is
eighty years old, at the outside. The lad travels to goodness knows where, goes around with suitcases full of
money, and she says, that one is a legitimate Assumpção.
But Assumpção money has always been clean, the money
of those who don't need money. You should know, ma'am,
that when President Campos Sales granted my father the
concession for the port of Manaus, he was a well-liked
young politician; his family fortune was old. I don't know
if I've ever told you that my great-grandfather was made
a baron by Pedro I of Brazil. He paid substantial taxes to
the Crown on the Mozambican labour trade. Though
today I am experiencing hardship, soon I will be sitting
in the lap of luxury; that's how it goes for those who deal

in large sums of money. I spoke to my lawyers just yesterday, and the compensation for the expropriation of my farm at the foot of the mountains is finally about to be paid. Governments have come and governments have gone, and the claim, for a petty amount that they decided upon off the top of their heads, has been working its way through the system for sixty years. The person who drew my attention to the outrage was my son-in-law, who wanted to see the old property where Maria Eulália had narrowly missed being born. I confess that, for me, it was somewhat depressing to see the ruins of the colonial farmhouse, the skeleton of the chapel, the charred stable, the dry grass and barren ground of the farm where I'd spent my childhood. The countryside was now overrun with factories, and a few favelas were already infesting the outskirts. But when Amerigo Palumba, who hadn't known the farm in all its splendour, arrived at the edge of the stream, he said, cazzo, this is paradise. At that moment, it is true, the stream was a sight to behold, with the sunlight slanting through its dense green waters, which then took on a mustard hue. And a gust of wind, perhaps coming from the direction of the cellulose factory, brought a sulphurous odour that made my pregnant daughter nauseous. But while the farm had been rendered useless for agriculture and leisure, its two thousand acres would be crucial for the new highway that was to be built. The experts hadn't considered that properly, I was told during a visit to the fancy law firm engaged by Palumba. Before he betrayed my trust, my son-in-law showed signs of a flair for business that, I have to admit, was never my forte. We had a few get-togethers at my chalet in Copacabana, where he visited me at night, bringing a bottle of whisky in a satin-lined box. He said he represented international finance groups, responsible for hefty investments in funds to rebuild Europe. His clients included friends of the Italian nobility, who, to make cash, didn't hesitate to sell their castles to eccentric American millionaires. It was obvious where Palumba was heading when he took his time examining the chalet, saw traces of termites in its wood, asked how large the property was. And Maria Eulália, beside him, didn't hesitate to slight the house in which she'd been born and raised, this ridiculous Swiss architecture in a tropical country. They suggested I sell the chalet to some developer and move in with my mother in the neoclassical mansion in Botafogo. At least I could comfort her with my presence, though she no longer recognized me. Mother's disorder had set in years earlier, with a kind of dysphasia. Her speech was clear and fluent, but her words were all out-of-order. And when she realized that no one understood her, she became irritable, switched to French and that was that. She scrambled her words in French too, but not only did her chauffeur Auguste understand her, he responded with words that were even more garbled. She called him Eulalie, and he, in his advanced dementia, happily answered to his former employer's name. And he'd sit with her in the drawing room, offer her his arm in the garden, allow himself to refer to her by her first name only, also Frenchified to Marie Violette. When Auguste died in her bed, wearing pyjamas with my father's monogram on them, Mother was widowed all over again, and her grief was more profound than the first time. By now she no longer spoke any language, nor would she move, or even cry, and I was moved to see her like that, her sadness finally crystallized. Meanwhile my enthusiastic daughter, with her bulging belly and hare-brained plans, urged me to deposit the family's future in Amerigo Palumba's investment portfolio. But because I didn't know how to part with Matilde's house, I began to consider sacrificing the Botafogo mansion, which was expensive to keep up with its dozen servants. To afford her lifestyle, Mother had little more than my Father's pension, because all she received from the division of the Montenegro estate were some National Treasury bonds of little value. I took a deep breath and, with a pang in my breast, authorized the Palumbas to sell the mansion. I saw to Mother's removal myself and travelled in the back of the ambulance with her, without taking my eyes off her dulled eyes. She and her nurse were installed in a side room of the chalet, where the south-westerly wind wouldn't bother her. But the next day, without fuss, she simply stopped breathing. And, I'll have you know, the doctor took her blood pressure before and after the move; stable, like a child's. He believed Mother still had many years in front of her, if vegetative ones. According to the gardener from the mansion, however, Mother was like a flower, which can wither when it is repotted.

14

If I can't go with you, I'll write you a cheque so you can buy a nice little dress, just as soon as the money's in my account. Don't be shy, because any shop assistant in an Ipanema boutique will be able to advise you quite as well as I could. You may laugh, but in my day they didn't even have boutiques; with my money you'd buy a length of fabric at a draper's and have a dressmaker copy a sketch from a French magazine. Wealthy women did what Mother did; she went to Europe every year with my father and brought back clothes for all four seasons. That was when she was younger, because after the age of thirty she gave up travelling with him and was happy enough to send him off with a list. But if, in an emergency, one needed an exclusive item, they could always go to the French ladies who sold haute couture from home, recently imported from the leading fashion houses. Father was a customer of these ladies, and days before his death I went with him to one such address. I returned there recently, little more than a year later, looking for a dress that would do justice to Matilde's figure without offending my mother. The lady proposed a sand-coloured tailored skirt suit, sober but cut to the knee, as racées girls of seventeen or so were wearing in Paris at the time. And although she was touched by the unexpected gift, Matilde was still reluctant to come. Nor did she want to take little Eulália in the bassinet because, quite apart from a slight, intermittent fever, the baby was afraid of old people. I should have seen it coming; Matilde would happily go anywhere that wasn't my mother's house. Less than a week ago she got all wound up about going to the cabaret with me, and now I wouldn't know what to say to Dubosc. For me to attend the dinner alone would have appeared as a slight to the Frenchman, on whom my professional success in part depended. Matilde finally gave in to my arguments, besides, she could, as always, leave the baby with her nurse, a black girl who was practically a member of the family. I'd known her almost her entire life, as she was the youngest sister of my pal Balbino, over at the foot of the mountains. Balbino himself stopped by the chalet the other day to see baby Eulália, and took the opportunity to bring us a basket full of mangoes from the farm. He had started to rather irritate me, because he was forever laughing at nothing, and went around in a pair of purple trousers that I've never seen on a man. But Matilde had taken a shine to him, ever since the day he saddled up the best horse on the farm for her. She was enchanted with the bay, and couldn't wait to ride again, as soon as her breasts weren't so heavy. Matilde's milk was plentiful; just now she filled two baby bottles before breastfeeding the baby. I liked to watch her nursing, and when she changed breasts, sometimes she would let me take a sip at the free nipple. As a result we were running a little late when we left, leaving the bottles with Balbina only as a precaution, because a dinner at Mother's wouldn't end any later than eleven. In my father's day, banquets at the mansion were famous all-nighters, bringing together politicians of all stripes and the most beautiful women in town. Torches blazed in the garden, the house smelled of lavender, even the statues had been bathed for the occasion, and as a boy I liked to wander through the silent, solemn drawing rooms, minutes before the party began. I liked owning those still immaculate spaces, just me with my shadows slipping across the marble, past waiters lined up like sentinels. But this dinner would be low-key, without either waiters or torches, because Mother was still in mourning, and it hadn't been easy to get her to agree to open the mansion for a simple engineer. Just as I imagine it hadn't been easy to swallow her pride to write letter after letter to the Company until she secured her husband's old position for her son. But when the guard opened the gate, I was surprised by all the lights in the windows, like a house filled with children. With the garden in darkness, the mansion seemed to float in the night, almost more imposing than in Father's day. Perhaps Mother wanted the French to see that, when all is said and done, the Assumpção household could hold its own. She was at the piano, which, since she had become a widow, she practised without a sound: merely brushing the keys with her fingertips, so as to honour my father and yet not forget Chopin. She sat with Matilde and me on the Louis XV sofa in the music room, where the butler served us champagne and Mother her lemonade. Sitting between the two of them, my posture was a little tense; the Louis XV sofa wasn't comfortable. We sat there for a while without speaking, the only sound being the pendulum of the large clock, waiting for Dubosc to arrive from his usual cocktail party at the French embassy. Mother loved the silence, and to emphasize it, she soon returned to the piano and her noiseless waltz. But when the clock struck ten she slammed the lid shut, summoned the butler with a little bell and ordered that dinner be served. Matilde jumped to her feet, as was her way, and planted herself in front of me to be admired, the sand-coloured dress against her sun-printed skin. I may well have undressed her with my eyes, in an manner of speaking, but this is where my memory plays a trick on me. I undress Matilde with my eyes, but rather than seeing her naked, I see the dress without her body. I see myself smelling the dress, caressing it outside and inside, shaking it out to see how the silk falls: I'll take it. In exchange for six hundred mil-réis, I take the package from a pair of liver-spotted old hands, and I think that's where I was going with this. I arrived at the speckled hands of the French lady, from whom I had seen my father buy a sky-blue dress with a full skirt the same week he was murdered. At the time I paid less attention to the dress than to the way my father seized it, smelled it, stroked it at length, shook it this way and that, and asked for it to be gift-wrapped. I had no reason to know that, the following night, the dress would attend the last big party at the mansion. Nor did I distinguish it from so many other blue outfits when it passed under my very nose, on the body of a woman entering the music room arm-in-arm with her husband. I did happen to notice the woman, her freckled shoulders and brown hair, much taller than her husband. The couple were heading across to greet my father, who was leaning on the piano with a drink in his hand, while a blind pianist played ragtime. I saw my father kiss the woman's hand and shake that of her husband, who then turned to a waiter. And I didn't understand why the woman ran her hands over her own body just then and smiled at my father, who stared at her very intently before quickly looking away. Only now, eighty years later, like an alarm in my memory, as if the colour of a tragedy were sky-blue, do I recognize on her the full-skirted dress that my father had bought the day before. That's it all right, no question, I'd even be able to recognize it inside out; my father had run his hand over it, outside and inside, front and back, just as the woman now runs her hand over it from top to bottom. And at this point the husband glances over at the woman, who smiles at my father, who looks at the woman, who looks at her husband, who looks at my father, who looks at the blind pianist, and the woman adjusts her hair. It is surely a crucial scene, but one I overlooked that night, in part because brunettes weren't exactly Father's thing. I left the room, went for something to eat at the buffet, and now my memory has failed me, where was I? I think I'm lost, give me your hand. Yes, I was at Mother's dinner, and the butler was beckoning me over with concerned gestures. In the still room, I found a dozen opened bottles of Burgundy, smelling of mould and rotting fruit, and realized that Father's reds, untouched in the cellar, hadn't survived Rio's summer. I asked him to get some beers from the Frigidaire, because although she didn't drink, it would distress Mother to see white wine served with red meat. Mother, Matilde and I had already enjoyed the hors d'oeuvres, the salad, the galantine, and had reached the legs of lamb, when Dubosc arrived. He came carrying two rather tired-looking roses, white for my mother and red for Matilde, and a cardboard plate of empadas, which mother told the butler to give to the servants. Desolate about his tardiness, he helped himself to some lamb and immediately began talking about the Xavante Indians his French friends were trying to contact. Matilde let out a brief whistle and asked if the Xavantes weren't head-hunters, like the ones she'd seen at the Pathé Cinema. She spoke in her elementary French, articulating the words as if dictating them, and Dubosc was amused. He said that he had seen all manner of things working for the Company, and spoke of typhoons in Polynesia and the malaria he had contracted in Madagascar. He enquired as to the origin of the lamb, magnificent, and without waiting for an answer indentified African influence in

78

the seasoning, as he did in everything else here in Brazil. To that, Mother retorted, in emphatic French, that the gravy was in fact made with herbes de Provence, grown in our garden by Auguste, the French chauffeur. Hearing that on lamb nights a fellow countryman became chef de cuisine, Dubosc didn't hesitate to leave the table to go and congratulate him. His voice rumbled away in the kitchen and his guffaws merged with a clap of thunder. There was a flash, the lights began to flicker, and Mother's lips moved as if she were praying on the inside. A bolt of lightning had struck the neighbourhood and, as often happened on stormy days, the power went out. The house fell silent, except for the sound of the pendulum in the drawing room and my mother's voice, which was finally audible. Like a Spaniard, Mother was saying, the man speaks French like a Spaniard; she didn't approve of the engineer's accent. The butler brought a candelabrum with eight candles and Mother rose to her feet; I took it and offered her my arm, but she declined the support and walked off ahead of me. I went through the drawing rooms lighting her way, her shadow fractured on the stairs. I followed her down the corridor and helped her get comfortable in her room. When I closed her door, I found myself without the candelabrum, and I stopped to wait for a flash of lightning to get my bearings. I felt my way along the wall to the stairs, and noticed candlelight and an insistent tapping coming from the front hall. With a shiver down my spine I thought of my father, the percussion of his spatula on the ebony case, but it was the butler tapping at the wall phone. There's no line, he said, and I took his candlestick, which shook a little in my hand. The flame went out near the front door, which must have been opened by the wind. I arrived in the dining room blind and whispered, Matilde, Matilde; I don't know why I was speaking in such a low voice. There was also whispering in the stillroom, where, by the light of candles stuck into bottlenecks, the staff were eating the empadas with spoiled wine. From the kitchen came muffled laughter, and I thought I heard Matilde whispering in French, hun-gry hu-man head hunt-ers. There I found her sitting with old Auguste on the floor at the foot of the oven, its wood now reduced to embers, sharing a tray of patisserie. I looked around and, without my asking, Matilde told me that he'd left with his French friends. Then the light came back on and a long aah was heard, like when a good film or a collective dream is interrupted.

15

I won't lie, I've had other women since her; some I took home. And when the nurse Balbina heard the racket we made, she'd take you down to the beach, even after dark, sometimes in the rain. I really had made an effort to find company elsewhere and had even visited brothels, but nothing had taken my fancy. Girls I knew from the garçonnière also took house calls, but I failed over and over. My desire for your mother remained alive: her memory assailed me in bed, in the shower, on the stairs, and I pretty much avoided the kitchen entirely. So I tried to draw women into the ambit of my desires, but it wasn't so easy. I didn't dare have whores in the bed I'd shared with your mother, and not all of the girls were willing to put on her clothes. Even the more uninhibited, as they sauntered around the bedroom dressed as Matilde, typically revealed themselves as frauds; they looked like thieves. With those who eventually did carry it off, I'd send them off in a cab as soon as possible, imagining that your mother was going to reappear without notice.

Because these few usually didn't agree to come back a second time, I quickly became a kind of hermit. I'd lock myself in my room, chain-smoking, and my consolation was leafing through the picture magazines that were coming into vogue at the time. I could see your mother in any photograph of a woman taken from a distance, strolling down Avenida Central, lying on a beach in the Northeast, riding in the pampas, and reclining in bed I satisfied myself while examining such images. To let some air into my life, I even considered inviting some friends around on Saturdays, to drink cognac, talk about sports, maybe get them together for a few hands of bridge as my father used to. But if I hadn't even made friends back in my student days, it would be that much harder now that I lived in a rather uninviting house. The truth is that without your mother, the once sunny chalet was going downhill. And no matter how many high-rises they built around it, it was always Matilde's shadow that I saw on it. I barely noticed you growing up; you grew up in the gloom of a haunted house. Now addicted to colour magazines, French ones, American ones, I neglected to spend time with you as I had in the early days, when your mother had first left us. In those days, I'd often wake up feeling restless and go to wake you to see what was left of Matilde in your face. It wasn't my imagination; Balbina also noticed that each day you lost another of your mother's features, and by then you'd already lost all of the original shape of her mouth, not to mention the black of her eyes and her cinnamon skin. It was as if, in the still of the night, Matilde stopped by to collect her things from her daughter's face, rather than her dresses from the closet or her earrings from the drawer. Even my mother, who typically didn't pay you much attention, was surprised to see how you were changing. The girl really is getting prettier, said Mother with absent-minded vanity, since you were looking more and more like her. Despite my affection for you, I didn't take you places out of a feeling of decorum; having you with me just didn't seem natural. From the nursemaid to the Portuguese grocer, everyone knew that when your mother ran off, she had gone without leaving a note or packing a suitcase. But abandoning a tiny, unweaned baby, so small you could tuck her under your arm, no one could understand it, it made no sense, it couldn't be. A woman won't even give up a husband so easily; she'll exchange him for another, and sometimes quickly, before she can change her mind, just as it pains her to get rid of an old dress when reviving her wardrobe. The only reason for a woman to abandon her child is if another child is tugging at her by the belly with the force of a lover. That's why, at first, even I wondered if your mother was with child when she ran off. Yes, it's possible that Matilde wouldn't have taken you if she were pregnant, if she was already carrying in her belly the child of the man who had taken her from me. Which would also explain her behaviour towards the end, when she started to push me away. Your mother turned away from everything, her milk dried up overnight, have I never told you these things? Then forgive me, forget it,

83

you should have said something, give me a kiss. I've probably been on a rant, and I'll happily go back to talking only of things you already know. If, with age, we tend to repeat episodes from the past, word for word, it's not weariness of the soul; it's diligence. It's for ourselves that we old folks always repeat the same stories, as if making copies of them in case they go astray. I don't know if I ever told you how I met Matilde at my father's memorial service, when she said Eulálio in such a way that not even the most sensual of actresses was able to reproduce in my bed. I'm also pretty sure I told you how I went to spy on her a day later, all bubbly at the entrance to her school, the darkest girl in her class. I began to meet her every day; I have a lifetime supply of memories of Matilde from the school foyer alone. Hence my surprise when you came into my smoky room without knocking, wearing a white blouse and navy-blue skirt; I don't think I'd seen you in the Sacré Coeur uniform before. You jumped on my stomach and hugged me, crying, because there was a rumour going around school that you were a beggar's daughter. It was awkward, I was spread-eagled across the bed, and your shoes were on my magazines, where exotic women passed themselves off as Matilde. And you sobbed without interruption because the other children had been teasing you; they'd even claimed that you'd been found by the Sisters of Charity in a rubbish bin. I recomposed myself, gathered up the magazines and said, now, now, sweetheart, now, now; I didn't know what else to say. I felt remorse for not having done your mother's

84

bidding when she had called a photography studio down-town, where we were to pose for photographs for a family album, the three of us. Matilde had every reason to complain; we didn't even have the classic wedding photo, but I'd kept putting off the studio, then everything derailed. Now, now, sweetheart, now, now. I was running my fingers through your fair hair, and there was definitely nothing left in you that one could point to, wow, that you got from your mother. Mildewed dresses in the closet and rusting costume jewellery in the drawer, which, while certainly mementos for me, weren't even vestiges of her for you. Then it occurred to me that Matilde's family must have at least one photograph of her as a child, perhaps a picture of her first Communion that you could show your school friends. Late in the afternoon I went to Mother's house, where she was taking afternoon tea with Matilde's mother, and I heard their whining voices in the winter garden: she... the places she went... the company she kept... the end she met... When I walked in on them they changed the subject and began to discuss the imminence of another war in Europe, the waves of refugees arriving in the country every day: in Copacabana, Maria Violeta, all you hear is German and Polish... they're all of the same extraction, Anna Theodora, they're all of the same stock. At the first opportunity I asked if Dona Anna Theodora had something to remember her daughter by, any photograph would do, just for a few days, but she lowered her eyes and tackled the sponge cake. Mother rang the bell and told Auguste to ready my car, because I was leaving. The next morning, I decided to take you to school, and you must remember because you were really excited: you had never been in my car before. But you insisted that I park a block away; arriving at school with your father would have been the end of the world. I watched you walking along with your satchel, your feet turned in a little, occasionally glancing over your shoulder, until you blended in on the pavement with mothers, nursemaids, governesses, drivers and droves of schoolgirls getting out of cars and off the tram. Once all the bustle had subsided, I walked through the school gate and by force of habit stopped for a few long minutes in the foyer, my old waiting post. I retraced my steps to the foot of the stairs and back ten years to relive the day I saw Matilde slide down the handrail, for which she got a week's suspension. I went up to the principal's office and asked to be announced to the mother superior as the father of third-grade pupil Maria Eulália. Notre Mère was delighted to receive me in private, since she hadn't yet had the pleasure of meeting either my wife or me at parent–teacher meetings. I made excuses; I was out of town on business for much of the year and, furthermore, I was a widower. As it happened, my wife had also studied at Sacré Coeur. Notre Mère looked sad to hear that a former pupil had died in labour at the age of seventeen, of eclampsia. She also felt for my daughter, in whom she had indeed observed a certain shyness at playtimes, dare she say a misanthropic temperament. And she agreed that it might be comforting for a young girl who'd lost her mother to hear stories from those who had spent time with her in that very building, and perhaps see her classroom, draw on her blackboard, sit at her desk. Slide down the handrail, I joked, and Notre Mère laughed, shaking her head. Except, Matilde, Matilde, frankly she didn't remember any Matildes. Matilde Vidal, I insisted, and the secretary Mère Duclerc, who had appeared to be dozing over her breviary, chipped in, Vidal? Bien sûr, and she reeled off the names of Matilde's six sisters: Anna Theresa, Anna Amélia, Anna Christina, Anna Leopoldina, Anna Isabel and Anna Regina. She too had difficulty remembering Matilde, but abruptly straightened up at her desk to consult her card index. In silent tête-à-tête with Notre Mère, I tried to decipher her frozen half-smile, her grey eyes staring at me, her placid countenance and her nervous fingers, addicted to the rosary beads. And there was no doubt in my mind that she knew everything, about me, about my rejected daughter and about her mother's eternal damnation. Voilà, said Mère Duclerc, handing me a photograph of the seconde class of 1927. There were a dozen pupils sitting with their hands crossed on their laps, in front of as many others standing, their arms stiff by their sides. They were Matilde's classmates, I knew their faces. But she wasn't there; maybe she had been suspended that day.

16

I'm hungry. The nursing staff here are spiteful, with the exception of that girl: her name's not coming to me right now. When she's not here, someone needs to attend to me. I don't need to be fawned over, I abhor overfamiliarity: all I want is neutral, professional care. Do me a favour and bring me my goiabada pudding, I'm hungry. I did tip my plate onto the floor, I won't deny it, and I'll do it again every time I find a sinew in my steak. Not to mention the fact that the food reeked of garlic; wait till my mother finds out. Wait till Mother smells me, when she gets back from church and discovers I've been given the servants' food. Because when the nursemaid has the day off it's always the same; no one is patient with me. But I'm hungry and I am quite capable of banging my head against the wall until someone brings me my pudding. And when my father asks about the bump on my head, I'll tell him that I get beaten up here almost every day. I'll tell him in French, so you'll all look like idiots and no one will contradict me. Father doesn't allow anyone to lay a finger on his son, except for him and Mother. And when he beats me with his belt or the back of his hand, he may draw blood or even break a tooth, but a child's head is out of bounds. I'll have you all know that Father keeps a whip there in the library, behind the Larousse Encyclopaedia. He showed it to me once, the plaited antelope-hide strap, the fleur-de-lys on the handle. It's no longer used, a family heirloom that he inherited from his father, my grandfather Eulálio. But when he gets back from Europe, if he hears that someone hit his son over the head, he'll crack that whip in every direction. He'll flog you all, men and women alike; he'll give you a hiding like the ones my grandfather used to give old Balbino. Balbino wasn't even a slave any more, but they say that every day he'd take off his clothes and hug the trunk of a fig tree, because he needed his arse lashed. And Grandpa would beat him with the flat side of the whip, without malice in his hand, more for the sound than for the punishment. If he had wanted to flay him, he would have imitated his father, who, when he caught runaway slaves, would whip them with great style. The whip would barely crack; it was only a whistling in the air that one heard. My great-grandfather Eulálio merely grazed the rascal's flesh with the tip of his whip, but the welt would last forever. He had got the knack from his own father, who had crossed the sea with the fleet bearing the Portuguese court, and when he wasn't lending an ear to the crazy queen, he would climb up on deck to teach lazy sailors a lesson. But that may have been something my great-

90

great-grandfather Eulálio invented so as to honour the whip that his father, the famous General Assumpção, had wielded in the Castilian campaign against Robespierre's France. To cut a long story short, my great-great-great-grandfather the general was the son of Dom Eulálio, a prosperous businessman in the city of Porto, who'd bought the whip in Florence to beat Jesuits with. That being the case, come to think of it, Father wouldn't waste his historic whip on a bunch of roughnecks. He would simply turn you all out into the street, and that would be the worst punishment, because you'll never find a job like this anywhere else. I'm not just saying that because of your wages that are never late, the house out back where you get drunk and masturbate, the food you devour, the day off once a fortnight and the Christmas bonus. I also say it because of the personal attention you receive from Mother, the small thefts she turns a blind eye to, the hand-me-downs she passes on still in good condition. She goes out of her way to ensure that you all attend Mass well dressed, and she arranged for the cook, who used to dabble in black magic, to be exorcized at the Church of the Candelária. You've all been vaccinated, and the only one of you not to have had a medical examination is my nursemaid, who thought it indecent. But I'm going to ask Father not to fire her because I feel sorry for her; she'll never like another child as much as she likes me. Nor will she let another boy play with her big black boobies like she lets me; she slaps me across the wrist but she lets me. When she thought I was too old for a nursemaid Mother

91

hired a German governess, but it was hopeless. The Fräulein didn't allow any hanky-panky: she tried to make me speak German and take exercise, but she couldn't handle me. She had a nervous breakdown and went back to Bavaria. Besides my nursemaid, I think I'm going to ask my father to spare the laundress, who's always laughing and could talk the hind legs off a donkey. When I see the basket of freshly laundered clothes, I piss on it with all I've got, and she washes it all again without complaining; she washes as she sings a polka, gyrating at the washtub. The laundress was a half-caste that mother had brought from the countryside, and now Father won't trust anyone else with his linen shirts, which, back in his Manaus Harbour days, he used to send to Europe to be ironed and starched. My father's a stickler for such things; it's not surprising that he has his suits, tails and dress coats sent to a Russian prince who made his name in Petrópolis as a drycleaner. And the Italian barber comes to our house every morning to shave him and trim his moustache; I've never seen my father with a hair out of place. Never a spot or a wrinkle on his clothes; he leaves his room every morning looking as immaculate as when he entered it the night before, and when I was younger I believed that he slept standing up like a horse. I was terrified of becoming a senator myself in the future, of having to sleep standing up and always appear like my father, upright and serious. That's why I'll never forget the day when, as he was leaving for work, he leaned over to kiss my mother, who was sitting at the table, and I glimpsed the tip of the whip through the back slit of his jacket. It was glorious, like seeing him in fancy dress, with a leather tail hanging out of his tweed jacket. I laughed uproariously and asked where he was going to play with that tail. What are you talking about, young man? he said, but Mother was already twisting around to inspect his back. So Father pulled the whip out through the top of his jacket, slapped his palm with it, thought for a moment and said, you never know with those anarchists. That night a secretary called to let mother know not to wait up for the senator. His Excellency would be tied up until the following day in continuous session, or in an emergency meeting at the Ministry of Health, or behind closed doors with President Pessoa, because the government was preparing for a flu epidemic even worse than the Spanish one. The second she hung up, Mother became electric: she started pacing around the house and went up and down the stairs about fifty times. During dinner she rang the bell for anything she could think of, complained about everything and had a fit when she saw two flies mating on the Valencia lace tablecloth. And when she finally appeared to have calmed down, I tipped over my plate of rice, beans, pumpkin and liver, dumping it all on the carpet. I hated liver and didn't care that Mother sent me to my room without dinner. She had no idea that, on nights when I was confined to my room, the nursemaid brought me a goiabada pudding in bed. I want my goiabada now, I'm hungry.

17

Pumping me full of medicine is pointless, lying here in this bed, just useless; without my wife I don't know how to sleep. She didn't say where she was going, and Matilde's never been one to venture out alone at night. It's too late for shopping, much less a doctor's appointment. Even her old school friends she only visits by day so she'll be home by the time I get back from work. In fact, she hasn't even had time for her friends since she had the baby. And soon the baby will wake up hungry; Matilde shouldn't be long. Though, come to think of it, she hasn't been breastfeeding lately, but soon, soon I'll see them bound to each other again, cooing and crooning. I've just remembered little Eulália dressed in a pinafore exactly like her mother's, a mini Matilde. Matilde laughed and laughed with the baby in her arms, and didn't even hear the honking outside. That was the day Dubosc showed up with a couple I had met at the ambassador's reception. The man was a doctor to the French community. I invited them into the chalet, because they had been up and down Copacabana Beach looking for a beach hut, without success. Matilde was coming down the stairs with the baby in her arms and greeted our guests with a nod. When she heard they wanted to change their clothes she showed them to the bathroom, then asked me to unlock the car so Balbina could load it with Maria Eulália's baskets. When I told her we weren't going to the farm any more, her eyes welled up immediately; she'd been looking forward to her first ride after the birth of the baby for so long. But Matilde is light-spirited, and on our way down to the beach she was already laughing and laughing, bouncing the baby, who was making her debut appearance in a swimsuit just like hers. She understood that it wouldn't be polite to abandon the French couple on an inhospitable beach, besides which, we'd have many other weekends to enjoy the farm. We didn't, as it turned out, but I couldn't have foreseen that Dubosc and his friends would become habitués of the chalet. And eventually we've resigned ourselves to their company, because, though they never wash their feet when they come back from the beach, they're really no trouble. They only make extra work for the cook, who has to make bigger lunches and restock our beach tent with lime cocktails every hour. This leaves Matilde free to play with the baby and nursemaid, while I entertain the couple, praising Rio de Janeiro's landscape, telling them of Phoenician inscriptions in the mountains and of hermaphroditic birds that inhabit the islands off the coast. I also talk about the French invasions, the dream of

France Antarctique, and have even invented a Breton forefather, Admiral Villegaignon's right-hand man. But the doctor always interrupts me to describe his activities in parts of the country that only he knows, in those jungles that foreigners like to plunge into. And he will go on about paludism, schistosomiasis, Chagas disease, Hansen's disease, and between one endemic disease and another I find myself gazing at the Forte de Copacabana, hoping an ocean liner will emerge from behind the rock. At midday Matilde takes Eulália home, where she feeds her and rocks her to sleep with the oogey-boogey-man lullaby. She returns to sit with me, makes me lay my head in her lap and says, open your mouth and shut your eyes. She fills my mouth with sand and races off so I'll chase her into the sea, then invites me to hunt sand crabs or play catch with her. I imagine the French expected a more demure wife, with certain intellectual attributes, for a man of my position. But Matilde almost never participates in our conversations, and brings the baby to the dining table, to my discomfort. It may be that I make her self-conscious with my laughter, on the rare occasions when she opens her mouth to speak French. I'm quick to correct her pronunciation, apologize for her grammatical errors, and so she'll often stop short in the middle of a sentence. I know she can get by without me, or she wouldn't have passed her first year of school. Nor would she and the doctor's wife understand one another. The wife has begun to frequent the beach on weekdays too, and talks about her adventures with her husband across

97

Latin America. As a result Matilde has got into the habit of telling me stories about Mexican peasants, or Indians who go naked in the snows of Patagonia, while I long for her in bed. Still in her nightgown, she makes me listen to the legends of Andean civilizations, delighted at their fertility rites. If she's actually interested in the civil war in Nicaragua witnessed by the doctor and his wife last year, I imagine Dubosc, who fought as a volunteer in the Great War, would leave her awestruck by his stories. He once told me that he had been a lieutenant in the French army and even mentioned a bullet wound sustained on the plains of Picardy, but then he dropped the subject. He must be embarrassed by some scar, which would explain why he never takes off his shirt at the beach; I've never seen him enter the water. Perhaps with his friends and my wife he is eloquent, maybe he even shows them the medal he says he was awarded in the war, but Matilde has never mentioned it to me. I wouldn't even have known that, in addition to the doctor's wife, Dubosc also visited my house at odd hours, if it weren't for the Company secretary. When I dropped by the office one Friday, after a day of bargaining at customs for clearance for some cannon barrels, I heard her joke that Monsieur Dubosc was already adapting to the Rio lifestyle and had taken the day off to go to the beach. That night Matilde didn't as much mention it, going into raptures over the baby, whose neck was growing stronger, and showing me how she could already hold up her head. I was staring at the sand in the cracks in the parquet flooring, and when I enquired about Dubosc, Matilde confirmed that he had stopped by to change his clothes, but that she'd barely seen him. It wasn't the first time; even the doctor showed up on occasion. According to her, whenever the French come together, they drink and laugh and jabber among themselves, and don't even stay for lunch. I found it curious that Dubosc had never mentioned these visits to me, but now I knew why he had missed a recent commitment at the Ministry of War. He was presumably sipping lime cocktails on the beach, while I waited for an audience with the minister, and was only seen after dark by his aide-de-camp. Admittedly, I didn't need Dubosc to schedule an artillery test to exhibit the new Schneider cannon barrels, which the minister was finally going to attend. Dubosc was already sceptical about such promises, but he nevertheless arranged to meet me at Marambaia, as he'd get a lift with the doctor and his wife, who wanted to see the place. I should have suggested that we all went in my car, because from Gávea Beach the road rises up through thick forest and can become a trap. Winding, narrow, and poorly signposted to boot; even those who have taken it before, like me, hesitate at each fork. Just now, after driving around the mountainside and back down to sea level, I found myself on a new slope that I didn't recall. I may well have lost my way, as I had been somewhat distracted ever since I set out. I had left home with Matilde on my mind, musing over the thought that she was hiding something from me. She wanted me to believe that, in my absence, Dubosc helped himself to the chalet purely, like a beach hut at a French seaside resort. She wanted me to believe that they had never bumped into each other coming or going from the house, that their eyes had never met during hours of sunbathing. Lying next to him on the beach, I find it hard to believe that she wouldn't be at all curious about such a worldly man, that she wouldn't want to know how many continents he had visited, how many languages he spoke, in how many battles he had fought, or even why he never removed that brown shirt from his body. No, Matilde wouldn't be able to resist engaging him in conversation; soon she'd be asking him about his life in France, if he were married, if his wife were young and beautiful, how many children they had. Dubosc might even have a daughter Matilde's age, and for him Matilde must be entirely without mystery: a native girl not unlike those he had met in Polynesia, her only distinction being that she can dance the maxixe. Yet, looking at Matilde belly-down in the sand, I doubt he's never entertained the thought of an occasional secret encounter in his hotel room, after months of paying for worn-out women in distasteful whorehouses. And it suddenly seemed obvious that the French had deceived me; they would never consider venturing alone down the steep, potholed road on which I was lost. In that heat, which they called Senegalese, they would already be lying in the shade of Matilde's tent, with the baby and the nursemaid. But Matilde isn't one to stay in the shade; every so often she goes for a dip, and at some stage she will always take a bucket and go looking for shells for the baby. So it's likely that, to pass the time, Dubosc will catch her up and walk with her along the water's edge. They'll stop here and there to pick up a shell, Matilde crouching, Dubosc stooping, reaching out his long arm. They won't speak, but Matilde may discover some meaning in the rattle of the shells, which she places and he throws in the bucket. When the bucket is full to the brim, it will be as if everything between them has been said, and they will continue on to the fort at the end of the beach, where Matilde will want to cool off. I can just see her setting the bucket down at Dubosc's feet and entering the sea in that way of hers, as if she were skipping rope. She'll come out of the water pulling her hair back, and Dubosc won't notice that a small wave has overturned the bucket she left in his care. Matilde will see the shells scattered on the sand by the backwash and she'll think her future might be drawn there, but Dubosc will scoop them up in his giant paw. She'll take the shells that he throws in the bucket by the handful, covered in wet sand, and wash them one by one. She will look inside each shell, peer into those abandoned houses. And Dubosc will look at the sky; from the sun's position he'll calculate that I should be arriving at Marambaia. By that time I had no idea where I was; there was no sun on my road, I drove on immersed in green shadow. I was already convinced I was going in the wrong direction, but the road had narrowed so much that it was impossible to turn round. I was stepping hard on the accelerator, the car was almost out of petrol; I hated the forest for my having entered it. When I came to a clearing, I caught sight of a mountain just like Corcovado, and that's exactly what it was. Structures could be seen at the top, where they said a statue of Christ was to be raised. There were cars parked in a square on my right; it was the Vista Chinesa viewing platform, but instead of turning back I turned off the engine and let the car roll downhill towards the city centre, where I could fill the tank. And soon they'll be heading back to the tent, Dubosc carrying the bucket and Matilde with an unfamiliar expression on her face. When she sees her, Balbina will press little Eulália to her chest and run to the house, where she'll give her expressed milk from a bottle. The doctor and his wife will also hastily take their leave, to allow the new couple the afternoon alone. And Matilde will sit side-by-side with Dubosc, because the tent's shade is scant when the sun is at its peak. At midday precisely I pulled up at the beach promenade. There were few people around; it was easy to make out our tent. It was a sky-blue circle, from a distance it looked like the full-skirted dress of the married woman with whom my father had had his last affair. I tried to run to the tent, but I ran as if in a dream, almost in place, because my shoes were filling with sand. Heavily, I drew closer to the sky-blue circle, and in its circular shade I saw shadows moving. A little further and I made out Balbina, who gave a start when she saw me, and the baby, who started crying. I asked where Matilde was, Balbina pointed towards the chalet, and from the gate I could already hear music. I thought it was a maxixe, but it was the samba she listened to every day now: cross, cross, cross your heart. The door of the house was wide open, and in the living room I came upon Matilde in her bathing suit, dancing with black Balbino. Yes, black Balbino; I couldn't believe it, but it was him. They didn't react when they saw me, they just kept on dancing and looking at me and smiling at me as if it were nothing. Balbino was wearing a pair of very tight purple trousers, his bottom bigger than his sister's, and seeing my wife in the arms of that spade was, for me, the greatest shame. His backside gyrated as he danced, Matilde laughed and laughed, and the singer sang in a girl's voice: then I'll kiss you in the cathedral of love. The scene was becoming unbearable; neither of them wanted to stop that disgusting dance, so I gave Matilde's phonograph a kick. Its turntable and arm flew through the air along with the disc, which shattered on the ground. Matilde looked at me in shock, Balbino ran with tiny steps. The telephone had been ringing for a while; it was Dubosc calling me from the Marambaia barracks. He asked what I was still doing at home if the minister of war was on his way to the spit, possibly accompanied by President Washington Luís. I set a new personal record from Copacabana to Marambaia, an hour and a half at top speed without any delays, in spite of the rain that caught me by surprise halfway there. By the time I arrived everyone had gone; the authorities had cancelled the test due to the bad weather. I drove back via the city centre, where I bought the latest model RCA Victor radio-phonograph and two albums with twenty-four discs of samba. Matilde was overwhelmed by the gift and forgave me; she was light-spirited. It was only days later that she closed herself off to the world and began to hide her body under the loose-fitting dresses Mother had given her some time before. And today she went out without saying where she was going; Matilde's never been one to venture out alone at night. So, naturally, I take off like a madman looking for her, but that's only going to happen in a while. It's strange having memories of things that have yet to happen; I've just remembered Matilde is going to disappear forever.

18

If you knew how much I like your visits, you would race to see me every day. You're the only woman who still holds me in regard; without you I would starve to death. Without you they would bury me like a pauper, my past would be erased, no one would record my saga. I'm not just saying this to sweet-talk you; that's all I need, to be fawning on nurses. I'm merely repeating what I told my lawyers. I've just given them instructions so that you won't be left with nothing if something should happen to me. I won't leave what's left of my estate to a daughter who had me admitted here against my will; even immobile I would be much better off at home. My pains were chronic; I could already predict when and where they would occur. But here I feel pains that aren't mine; I must have caught a hospital infection. And while they used to cart me off for CAT scans for any reason, now that I really am in need there's no one to examine me. My bills must be overdue; I've heard rumours that I'm to be sent to a public hospital. If that is the case I will need your help, because you surely know of a more reputable care home. There used to be one run by Carmelite nuns in Botafogo. At a traditional institution my name would open doors, in contrast to this dump, where they extort money from us without any concern for its origin. Because my great-great-grandson deals in narcotics, you know. I think I saw him and his girlfriend on TV the other day, handcuffed at an airport, hiding their faces. If he winds up behind bars, then Maria Eulália will really let me go to seed. That's because she's not aware that I still have means. If she did she'd have squandered them already, as she squandered the mansion, the chalet and all of the furniture; she even hocked the family mausoleum. I wouldn't have left the chalet for all the money in the world, though I knew all too well that my wife's absence was permanent. But somewhere else I might not have heard her sighs; at that address she still came to see me in dreams. And I pretended to be offended by the offers that came in, chased off the estate agents that came to pester me at my daughter's urging. Maria Eulália couldn't accept that we occupied such a valuable piece of land in Copacabana, yet couldn't afford a car, a cook, a nursemaid for little Eulálio. By the time she was an adolescent she thought houses with yards were for hicks and envied her friends who were moving into the district's modern buildings, with their marble art-deco façades. Besides which, she used to say, I think it's creepy to live in the house where Mother died. It always shocked me to hear her talk like that, even though it was I who had invented the story that her

mother had died in our bed as she gave birth to her. It had
seemed like a good story at first, one that might give my
daughter mettle, at the same time that it afforded her
mother a triumphant exit. Sooner or later I'd have to
undeceive her, but I kept putting it off, and not only did
Maria Eulália grow up clinging to my charitable lie, but
she also improved on it herself. I can just see her school
friends trying to keep a straight face as she told them of
the nurses scurrying back and forth, the obstetrician in
despair and her mother in convulsions, frothing at the
mouth and imploring God to save the baby. I'm now convinced that Maria Eulália never entirely believed the
things she said; her talk of her dead mother was like
warding off evil, like knocking on wood. I think she came
down the school stairs trembling in her shoes every day,
fearful that a penitent mother might appear. Being met
by her sobbing mother in front of everyone, would have
been more mortifying for her than if a poor relative in
rope sandals had come to collect her. And the school
entrance was a social occasion for her final-year peers,
who paraded through the hall in high heels in front of
boyfriends and suitors. But of all of these, the most
desired, because he was a grown man, the friend of mar-
quesses and business partner of bankers, was inexplicably
attracted to the girl who sidled out with her head down,
keeping close to the walls. Amerigo Palumba began to
bring Maria Eulália home in his convertible, quoted
Italian poets, and gave her a book entitled Cuore. Not
knowing with what words to repay him, one day she

hesitantly told him the only beautiful story she knew. And after narrating the final moments of eclampsia, rictus, her mother's staring eyes, she was comforted by her first kiss on the lips. A sensitive man, she told me, you should see what a sensitive man he is. Even after they were married, Palumba would lavish her with affection whenever she remembered her story, and it must have been in one such embrace that little Eulálio was conceived. But no sooner had the mansion been sold than the bounder ran off with the proceeds, and Maria Eulália refused to believe that she had been ditched in such a vile manner. She preferred to put it down to her own dishonesty, to think that he had gone into exile when he lost confidence in her, because she had deceived him from day one with her fanciful tales. She was sure he'd caught wind of the rumour that had gone around when she was at school, according to which her mother hadn't died of eclampsia at all, but had run off, leaving behind a wimp of a husband and a babe-in-arms. Now, now, sweetheart, now, now, I said with a cigarette in my mouth, looking for matches. She was also convinced that Amerigo had run into Matilde in person at the door to her apartment; she suspected her mother of lurking around her Flamengo palace in the sky, as she had previously spied on her at the school gate. So I took her hands in mine, looked her in the eye and confessed that Matilde really had left home when she could barely crawl. But she had died only a short time after, in a car crash on the old highway from Rio to Petrópolis, and it was time that we let her soul rest in peace. On All Souls' Day I took Maria Eulália to Cemitério São João Batista, and we left white carnations at the family mausoleum, where, in bronze letters, were the names of my father, my mother and Matilde Vidal d'Assumpção (1912–1929). And I don't know why I hadn't made things clear to her sooner; from that point on my daughter was visibly more accepting of things. She gave birth serenely, breastfed little Eulálio for a year, and reminded me of Matilde in her maternal devotion. Later she went through a phase of unusual extroversion, spent hours on the phone, made herself up, attended vernissages, met a painter with whom she stayed up late talking in the drawing room. She and this young woman would leaf through art books, and from the top of the stairs I would hear the sound of pages being turned and the occasional word murmured by the painter: expressionism... Cézanne... Renaissance... And I may have misheard, but I think I also caught words whispered by Maria Eulália: eclampsia... spasms... save the baby... In the beginning I actually liked that the painter would dine with us, because it was the only time Maria Eulália prepared anything besides fried eggs or rice. But in time she began to take liberties, offering decorating tips for the chalet and claiming that the baroque desk I'd inherited from my mother was a shoddy fake. When she saw the oil painting of my grandfather in its rococo frame, she had a fit of laughter and said, that's what the Germans call kitsch art. She started sleeping over and I'm not sure if it was because of that that little Eulálio grew irritable, screaming and crying day and night. To drown his cries, the painter would turn the volume right up on Matilde's radio; I hadn't even realized it still worked. Eventually she brought over her belongings, her paints and canvases, converted the drawing room into her studio, and I resigned myself to it all because I didn't want to upset Maria Eulália. My daughter actually had a different colour about her, her eyes were sharper, and it was lovely to see her like that. She would have been perfectly happy if it weren't for the chalet, which the painter claimed had a bad vibe. So I gave in and sold the house of all my dreams. The building company paid us with two three-bedroom apartments, side by side on the eighth floor of a block behind our land. I kept the old furniture, Grandpa's portrait, and, after some hesitation, I also took the wardrobe with my wife's dresses and the nightstand with her jewellery in the drawer. The two of them decorated their apartment with curving armchairs and tables with tapered legs. Maria Eulália even bought a console with a Telefunken phonograph: she who had never been one for music. Now she listened to jazz as the painter created collages on black canvases, and little Eulálio, who suffered from asthma and allergies, spent hours in my apartment. He spent quite some time with me when my daughter took the painter and an art dealer from São Paulo to the United States, where there was supposedly a market for experimental work. After a few months Maria Eulália returned alone, and I moved my mountains of picture magazines into the laundry area to declutter a room just for her, since her apartment had been seized by the federal bank as collateral on colossal debts. No mention was made of the painter and my daughter was quiet for a long time, but I learned to appreciate her silent company. Without speaking, I would study her, observe her antiquated beauty, her paleness, the perennial dark circles under her eyes, her long face like my mother's. And I wondered whether she hadn't tortured herself from a young age, imagining that I wanted to see a replica of Matilde in her. When she was a little older, I'll never forget her look of astonishment when I kicked her out of my room after catching her trying on an orange tailleur of her mother's, which, apart from anything else, sat askew on her. And maybe her recent outbursts of happiness had been a kind of ungainly exhibition, like an owl venturing out in the sun without really understanding what was expected of it. Maybe Maria Eulália even blamed herself for having been born a girl, assuming that I had hoped for an heir. But even if that were the case, she'd already made it up to me with little Eulálio, who'd become a son to me. For him I even remembered old berceuses; I was happy to croon softly when he climbed into my bed in the middle of the night, frightened by something. I taught him to read and obtained a scholarship for him at my old Catholic school, where my name still opened doors. I grew attached to the boy, who, notwithstanding the Palumba in his name and his somewhat rustic features, was definitely of my stock. He would accompany me to second-hand bookshops in the city centre and help me dig out photographs from the turn of the century, back when the Assumpção family called the shots in this country, as I taught him. It was he who found a photo from 1905 showing my father, the young senator, wearing a top hat among President Rodrigues Alves's retinue. I took him in short trousers to the Senate, had him photographed at the lectern where his great-grandfather had spoken so many times. The child always had his nose buried in history books and his report cards filled his mother with pride. Versed in politics from an early age, by the time he started high school he was able to debate the country's perilous predicament with his teachers, as their equal. And one day he came to inform me that he'd become a communist. So be it, I said to myself. If communism comes to power, Eulálio d'Assumpção Palumba will probably make it onto some politburo, or a council of ministers, if not the party's central committee. But instead of communism, we had the 1964 military coup, so I reminded him of our old family ties with the armed forces. I even showed him the whip that had belonged to his Portuguese great-great-great-great-great-grandfather, the famous General Assumpção. But at that tender age, Eulálio was still vulnerable to the influence of the unwise, perhaps even of red priests. Either that or his hot Calabrian blood went to his head; all I know is that he decided that he was going be a hero of the resistance. He brought home a mimeograph, printed pamphlets: in vain I tried to explain to him that heroism is vulgar. One night he stuffed his

112

junk into some backpacks and my daughter went into a panic, saying he had left to go into hiding. A short time later, seven police agents invaded our apartment, ransacked everything, shook Maria Eulália, asked after someone by the name of Pablo, and I told them there had been a misunderstanding: the boy was an Assumpção of fine stock. I even showed them the portrait of my grandfather in its gilded frame, but a goon clouted me over the ear and told me to stick my grandfather up my arse. The same boor scattered my collection of photos across the floor, and it wouldn't have done me any good to protest when he confiscated the Florentine whip. Some time later we received a phonecall telling us to go fetch a child from the army hospital; it was Eulálio's son by a comrade of his who had given birth while in prison. This new Eulálio I raised as if he were my son, taught him to read, enrolled him at the Catholic school where my name opened doors, had him photographed in short trousers at the Senate. From day one he proved to be a sharp pupil, interested in the history of Brazil, debating with his teachers as their equal, and one day he became a communist. My daughter says he was killed in prison, but no one knows for sure; all I know is that one day I received a phone call telling me to go collect his son from the army hospital. This new Eulálio I raised as if he were my son, taught him to open doors, had him photographed in short trousers with red priests, but the medicine tasted strange. I don't like the way you're looking at me; I don't recognize that caustic smile of yours. I have a burning sensation in my oesophagus; you made me drink that soda and now I'm close to death. Get on with it, don't just stand there watching me in agony, at least give me my morphine.

19

You knocked me down, but I picked myself up, you messed me around, but I'll never give up; I like hearing the laundry woman singing downstairs. Today I had a visit from Father, who never comes to my room. He stopped by to tell me to lie still in bed, otherwise the mumps will travel down to my testes, my scrotum will swell up and my dick will turn inside out. That's why I'm not turning my head to look at you, but out of the corner of my eye I can see you in a dressing gown and slippers, pummelling the air. It's the thermometer and you're shaking it before placing it under my armpit, then sitting on my bed and pressing the back of your hand to my neck and forehead. If it were up to me I'd get sick more often; I'd have the mumps again, and chicken pox and the measles and appendicitis. And my room would be constantly lit by this warm lamplight, with the windows closed even by day. And when you sang me a berceuse, I'd glimpse a tear quivering in each of your eyes, the same pair of tears as when you play the piano, and I'll stop here so I don't bore you with sentimentality. Outside of music, you always dam up your feelings so nobly, though they no doubt cause you pain, as clogged milk-ducts must cause pain. You've also told me that you don't like people who greet those they barely know with kisses on both cheeks, who pat backs and touch others as they speak. At Father's party I noticed you only smiled at that woman who was pretending to be your friend, whispering in your ear and gesticulating and laughing too much, to be polite. You probably don't even remember; she had freckles and brown hair and walked up to you when the waiters were serving the petits fours. Then she excused herself, kissing you on both cheeks, and went over to a handsome fellow who looked like Rudolf Valentino, who was sitting in an armchair drinking whisky. But when the fellow stood I was surprised by his low stature; he reminded me of a caricature from the magazine Fon-Fon, his torso dispro-portionate to his short legs. They left side by side, and that was when I registered that it was the couple from the music room. I had seen them only a little earlier with Father. But someone has suddenly opened the blinds, and with the sun in my face I can't see a thing. My mother has disappeared; she was just here with me. If someone finds her, please ask her to come back to talk to me, it's impor-tant. I repeat, if anyone is listening, go to my mother's room for me, urgently, because I've got the mumps and I'm not supposed to move. And if she's in her wheelchair, with a crazy look on her face and talking in French, don't worry, go ahead and open the middle drawer of the jacaranda desk. Look carefully, because somewhere at the bottom you'll find a photo the size of a standard sheet of paper, dated 1920 on the back. But don't forget to also bring me the magnifying glass, which is in a smaller drawer, because I need to check something. I could almost swear that that Rudolf Valentino is there on the stairs of the Guanabara Palace during a congressional visit to King Albert of Belgium, who was staying as a guest there. It's one of Mother's favourite photos, and shows my father next to Queen Elisabeth, a step below the king. Matilde's father's head is also there, a little further back, and perched on the very top step, if I'm not mistaken, is the short fellow with brilliantine in his hair. I really need the photo so I can point him out to Father, if he happens to come by again. Man to man, I might be able to convince him not to get involved with Rudolf Valentino's wife. I'd try to dissuade him from buying that sky-blue dress, but of course he wouldn't let me finish my sentence. Don't rock the boat, Lilico, he'd say, go fly a kite, and in the end he would die as he was destined to die, in his garçonnière with six bullets in his chest. And even if he did listen to me, he might walk straight into the ambush anyway. Because he might have sensed that times would soon be different, and my father would never willingly remain in an era that didn't belong to him. His offshore fortune was about to evaporate, and I can't imagine him without his annual trips to Europe, his first-class women, restaurants, hotels and ship's cabin. In politics, civility was to give way to fanfaronade and

117

exhibitionism; I don't see my father campaigning for votes, climbing up onto podiums, shaking hands with commoners, smiling for photographs in dirty clothes. Le Creusot & Cie. no longer enjoyed the prestige of its early days, when the French military mission was first installed in Brazil. We were now the subject of frequent attacks in the press, and I also had to put up with Dubosc, snorting and muttering merde alors after every line I translated for him. Even O Paiz lampooned us in its editorials, cartoons poked fun at our artillery, depicted as scrap left over from the Great War. And day after day we lost ground to our competitors, who didn't hesitate to seduce certain journalists, with whom we'd exchanged favours just the other day. It ended up contaminating the atmosphere in the office. The secretary confided that Dubosc had actually gone as far as to ask her for a list of the people I spoke to on the phone. He was no doubt afraid that I'd change allegiances, or perhaps even sell on confidential information. Dubosc didn't know me and was within his rights to question my integrity. And likewise, I don't even know who his father was; I'm not aware of the Dubosc lineage. But while I considered the Company almost as a paternal legacy, he was only attached to it by commercial ties. He wouldn't have had the scruples to resist more attractive offers. Indeed, while he had previously only gone to the beach sporadically, or to hunt capybara on the occasional weekday, he now mysteriously disappeared every single day. He could only have been in bed with our rivals. And one Friday when he headed off before noon, wishing us a good weekend, I lost my patience, let the secretary go home early and called it a day myself. I then regretted my rashness, in part because I didn't have anything to do with my afternoon off. I ordered a coffee at a patisserie and lit a cigar so I could watch the world go by. I even saw two former classmates of Matilde's whom I knew by sight pass by. I think they saw me too and I made as if I was going to stand, but they quickened their step and ducked into an arcade. I wandered down Avenida Central a little longer before going to fetch my car, and stopped at a florist on my way home. I don't know if Matilde would have come down to the living room if I'd invited her friends over. But I doubt it; she no longer answered when I knocked on her door. It is possible that she was even inappropriate with the doctor's wife, who never returned to take a dip in the sea. Matilde became increasingly reclusive, shutting herself up in the side room of the chalet, which was actually a junk room full of bric-a-brac and an old divan, where perhaps she lay, catatonic, for hours on end. She kept to no set meal-times, heating her food herself and eating in the kitchen without speaking to anyone. When the crisis began she still kept an eye on her daughter, now not even that. I think she was hurt when she caught little Eulália clinging to the wet nurse's breast. When a mother's milk dries up suddenly like that, said the nurse, it's because she's lost someone close, or suffered a great disappointment in love. She looked upwards when she referred to someone close, and disappointment in love she said

119

looking at me, as if I were a bad husband. Me of all people, who missed Matilde as much as my daughter did, and had no other breasts to console me. I did everything in my power to bring her back into the world; just now I bought an armful of red arum lilies to brighten up the drawing room. Matilde loved the petals of the arums, so scarlet; they reminded her of plastic hearts. I searched everywhere for a vase for the flowers, with no one to help me. On the stove there sat pans of cold rice and beans. The cook was no doubt flirting at the grocer's, while the nursemaid sashayed round the square with little Eulália. I found the vase among spiders' webs in the pantry. The furniture was dusty, the entire house in need of its mistress's eye. And as I was arranging the arum lilies in the living room, I was surprised to hear Matilde crying quietly; unburdening herself from time to time could only do her good. I was already on my way to offer her help, but halfway up the stairs I paused to listen more closely to her moaning. I will not go so low as to betray Matilde's privacy here, but I can say that every woman has a secret voice, with a characteristic melody, only known to those who take her to bed. That was the voice I heard there, or wanted to hear; it had been weeks since I had lain with Matilde. And I savoured the thought that at that moment she was caressing herself and thinking of me, just as I loved her in my mind every night in my room. I reached the top of the stairs treading lightly. Under no circumstance would I interrupt her; I wanted to watch her in secret to the end. But suddenly, out of the blue, I felt a violent hot rush to my head and my skin tightened all over. I was abruptly seized by the idea that there was a man with Matilde; I could already hear a man's panting mixed with her moans. It was as if my eyes had filled with blood, and the blocks of the parquet floor imitated the footprints of a big man, sandy feet on the path to Matilde. I saw footprints all over the floor, old and recent, right feet and left feet, coming and going, sideways too; a jigsaw puzzle of juxtaposed footprints. I thought I was going to burst in on them shouting, chase the scoundrel out and beat my wife's face in. But no, I found myself stealthily following Matilde's languid lament; I now needed to spy on her even more urgently than before. I crossed the empty rooms, hearing sobs and running water in the bathroom, and I don't know why but somehow surprising Matilde cheating on me in our bed would have diminished me less than the sight of her on her feet, giving herself to a wet man. I reached the half-opened bathroom door breathless, and saw Matilde doubled over the sink as if she were vomiting. For a second it occurred to me that she might be pregnant, then I saw her bare right shoulder, where she had let down one side of her dress. I ran to embrace her, ashamed at having judged her so unfairly, but she brusquely straightened her dress and slipped past me, leaving the tap running. I saw milk spattered around the edge of the sink, the air smelled of milk, there was milk leaking onto your mother's dress; have I never told you this story? Then ignore it, best take what I say with a pinch of salt; you know how I'm given to fancies. I'll happily go back to telling you only of the good times I spent with Matilde, and please correct me if I get confused from time to time. We old folks tend to repeat episodes from the past, but never with the same precision, as each memory is already a copy of a previous one. Even Matilde's face; one day I realized I was starting to forget it, and it was as if she was leaving me all over again. It was agony: the more I tugged at her memory, the more her image unravelled. All that was left of her was a few colours, the occasional glimpse, a fluid memory. My thinking about Matilde was vague in form; it was thinking about a country rather than a city. It was thinking about the tone of her skin and trying to apply it to other women, but as time went by I also forgot my desires, tired of the picture magazines, lost all sense of a woman's body. By that time your mother no longer came to me in dreams, I no longer rolled over in sleep to wake up on the right side of the bed, where the mattress was still concave from her. And when we downgraded, I was able to share my double bed with you without any risk of crying out Matilde, Matilde, Matilde, or muttering improprieties in the middle of the night. Even living in a one-room dwelling, in a déclassé district, on the noisiest street of a dormitory town, even living like a Hindu outcaste, not once did I lose my composure. I wore silk pyjamas bearing my father's monogram, and never went without a velvet dressing gown to the outhouse, where I tended to my personal hygiene in a bathroom with unfinished walls and a cement floor. Bathing was hard work, as there was only a capricious pipe for a shower, which at times dripped water as if from a pipette, and at others spurted jets of water all over the toilet. And it was in these circumstances that I had a late and maybe even final vision of Matilde, like a last rally before death. Standing under a ribbon of water, I was transported back to our old bathroom in the chalet, dreaming of its generous shower. Facing the gritty wall, I was dreaming of the seahorses on the tiles and the English porcelain, when without any effort I remembered Matilde from head to foot. She appeared to me in her seventeen-year-old body under the gushing hot water, pulling her hair back and squeezing her eyes shut so she wouldn't get soap in them. I remembered her enveloped in steam, now opening her black eyes wide at me, I remembered her demure smile on her lips, the way she used to raise her shoulders and beckon to me with her index finger, and for a second I thought she was summoning me to the other world. I remembered her body movement as she leaned against the seahorses on the wall, the subtle shift of her hips, and suddenly I was possessed of a force I hadn't felt in years. I looked down at myself in astonishment; there was in my old man's body a desire for Matilde comparable to when we first met. I don't think I ever told you how I first saw her at Father's memorial service. Standing next to me, you must have noticed me fidget, I wouldn't be surprised if you had glanced at my crotch and immediately looked away in disbelief. And although you were surrounded by absolutely everyone, since even the

Vice-President of the Republic had come to offer you his condolences, you were forced to pay attention to your future daughter-in-law. She was the darkest in her row, and in her Marian habit she was truly a provocation, almost obscene, enclosed in vestments. Because with her eyes alone, those Moorish eyes, Matilde hinted at her slightest body movements, the subtle shift of her hips, and I had to hurry home, in need of a cold shower. And in the shower I observed my quaking body, but my mind has just failed me and now I'm not sure which shower I was talking about. My memories, and memories of memories of memories, are so numerous that I'm not sure in which layer of recollection I was just now. I don't even know if I was very young or very old, all I know is that I looked at myself almost fearfully, bewildered by the intensity of my desire. And I had the absurd impression that it was my father's hard cock in my hand, but it's sad when you're abandoned, talking at the ceiling like this, burning up with the mumps. You forgot my kiss, didn't take my temperature and left without singing me my berceuse.

20

You're going to be bowled over, seeing as how no one believes how old I am, but that old girl isn't my mother; she's my daughter. She came to check up on my health, so as to arrange for my speedy discharge. When the people here see my empty bed tomorrow, many will make the sign of the cross, assuming the worst. But don't worry about me, because I'll be eating grapes in Copacabana, in a room with a view of the beach. Probably in a wheelchair, but one of those motorized ones, so I can go out on my own whenever I feel like it. I was somewhat resistant to the idea of living in an apartment building; it seemed promiscuous. But the convenience of it finally broke down my resolve. Don't hesitate to look me up sometime; I'll leave you my card. The building has a certain class, with a would-be art-deco foyer, discreet neighbours and doormen who wash. In short, it's a selective environment, so I was naturally surprised when a big chap with the flat nose and thick skin of a Northerner came into the lift with me. I indicated the service lift to him, but he turned his back on me and pressed the button for my own eighth floor. Upstairs, Maria Eulália laughed uproariously over the incident: according to her, I was the only person in Rio de Janeiro who didn't know Xerxes. Even my grandson had a trading card of the veteran Fluminense centre half, which has just reminded me that I don't live in Copacabana any more and haven't for some time. To give my daughter more privacy, we traded our apartment for two smaller ones in Tijuca, with windows overlooking the Maracanã. Closer to work, said Xerxes, who hadn't actually played for a while as a result of a knee injury. He did strike me as somewhat overweight, and his face was full, but he claimed he was anxious to start training again. He considered himself hard done by and believed Brazil would have won the World Cup in 1950 if the coach hadn't passed him over for an absolute donkey. He had been disciplined in 1954, but was sure to be on the squad for the 1958 Cup and promised my grandson he'd bring him a trophy from Sweden. Meanwhile he went out with my daughter every night, Eulália in red lipstick and Xerxes always dressed up; each week she would buy him a tie, or some moccasins, or a gabardine suit. And for me, enjoying the late afternoon breeze as I explored a less affluent part of town was a novelty; sometimes I'd even walk as far as the city centre. I would also stroll through Parque Quinta da Boa Vista, though I was sad to see how the former Imperial Palace, which my grandfather had frequented so often in the days of Pedro II, had been allowed to fall into disrepair. At dusk I'd return along the poorly lit paths, where there was no risk of running into anyone I knew. In Copacabana people were beginning to turn their noses up at me for allowing a half-caste football player under my roof; furthermore I had been receiving a series of complaints from the residents' committee about the shouting in my apartment at night. Xerxes was in the habit of beating up my daughter when he drank, yet in working class neighbourhoods such scenes are commonplace; no one is scandalized by them. On turbulent nights like those Eulálio would come and stay with me, and I'd even reserved the spare room for him, as he was too big for my bed. I didn't foresee that Maria Eulália would also end up joining us, after Xerxes almost cut her throat with a razor. That thug continued to live across the hall from us and entertained lady friends in Maria Eulália's apartment with all-nighters of liquor, bolero and beatings. And when a court official turned up with an eviction notice, he responded with bullets. He only agreed to hand over the keys in exchange for half the value of the property, which my daughter sold to cover her overdraft. Such developments, painful as they were, had the effect of reuniting our family; Eulálio was visibly comforted to see his mother lying quietly in a bed next to his. And feeling his presence night after night, as he pored over his books by the light of the bedside lamp, she naturally grew more and more fond of the child. But she didn't interrupt him with maternal chatter, pester him with kisses and caresses, or worried looks; I actually believe that Maria Eulália loved her son with her sense of

127

smell. And she took leave of her senses when he took off into the world and changed his name. They say Eulálio was fearless, he left determined to face the armed forces. Maria Eulália never slept properly again; she went out every morning looking for bad news and only came back late at night with terrifying rumours. One night, well after midnight, I heard a commotion at the door and was about to call the police, thinking it was Xerxes, wanting to beat up my daughter for old time's sake. But it was the police; twenty special agents broke down the door, made a mess of everything, shook Maria Eulália and insulted me. And the poor thing, who was already a bundle of nerves, froze before my eyes the day the phone rang for me, for no one ever called me. A Colonel Althier asked if it was really me, Assumpção, addressing me with a certain camaraderie. Colonel Adieu? I asked. The line was dreadful, full of static. Althier! Colonel Althier! said the man. He wanted to know if I was related to a Eulálio d'Assumpção Palumba. He's my grandson, I said, my only grandson, and the colonel congratulated me; he had good news for me. Good news, I repeated, and Maria Eulália began to tremble from head to foot, her hopes of getting her Eulálio back were resuscitated. But the colonel's congratulations were for Eulálio's son, who had just been born at the army hospital; nineteen and a half inches, seven and a half pounds. The baby was to be entrusted to his closest living relatives, since the mother, known only by assumed names, had unfortunately died in childbirth. For me, the arrival of the baby was unquestionably good

128

news, though a great-grandson will always seem at once familiar yet so strange, like the local river miles downstream. But Maria Eulália was the child's grandmother, and we all know that grandmothers are like overenthusiastic mothers. Not Maria Eulália. Perhaps because she'd received the news on the wrong foot, she took it as an outrage and saw the child as a decoy. In her mind, they were giving her a boy as if in barter, or like hush money to compensate for the disappearance of the other one. Maria Eulália didn't even want to go to the hospital with me; if it had been up to her, the baby would have remained there. But I persuaded her that we could reach Eulálio through the kind colonel. Until then the authorities most certainly had no idea that they were dealing with such an important family. Once we had confirmed our suspicions that Eulálio was being held in a basement somewhere, subject to possible discomforts, it was clear that he would promptly be released. We would also be informed of any accident that might have befallen him, which was everyone's worst fear, but off the top of his head like that the colonel couldn't say for sure. He said he would call, but Maria Eulália wasn't convinced; she moved her grandson's cot into my room and didn't even see fit to feed him. It fell to me to prepare the powdered milk for his bottle, which gave him colic and dysentery; he became dehydrated and I spent a fortune on paediatricians. But nothing moved his grandmother, not even his resemblance to his father or his bulbous Palumba nose, which she viewed as just another instance of fraud. I thought she'd be pleased when I had the baby's birth certificate issued in the name Eulálio d'Assumpção Palumba Junior, after his father. But she only referred to her grandson with pronouns: he's a pain, he smells. My daughter had lost much of her delicacy after she fell in with a bad-tempered crowd. One day she came home with a woman in sandals with dishevelled white hair. They went into my room without asking, opened the wardrobe, and took Matilde's dresses off their hangers one by one. Fuck yeah, said the old girl, fuck yeah, and from her voice I recognized my daughter's friend, a painter who was now in the theatre. She wanted to put on a liberal play, but set it in the 1920s in order to evade the censorship of the time, and thought the dresses would make good costumes. That was too much. I told the painter to be off and with Maria Eulália I was firm; exposing my wife's clothing on stage would be an affront to her memory. But Maria Eulália insisted, claiming that her mother's possessions were as much hers as they were mine. Besides which, she said, it's bad luck to keep a schizophrenic's dresses in one's home. That's always the way it goes, like Chinese whispers; someone had told Maria Eulália that her mother had ended her days in an insane asylum. So I took her hands, looked her in the eye and told her that when Matilde had abandoned us, she had gone in secret to a sanatorium in the countryside, where she soon died of tuberculosis. She had had herself admitted under another name so the public health department wouldn't put her daughter, Maria Eulália, in quarantine, which is

130

what they did with the children of consumptives back then. Speaking of which, we could go visit her grave at Cemitério São João Batista. But Maria Eulália was heading out to her first rehearsal: she had taken it into her head to become an actress. And the painter was already on her way up to help her carry off Matilde's dresses; she also took my grandfather's portrait, which she thought would give the stage set a touch of burlesque. Maria Eulália began to devote entire days to rehearsals and would lock herself in her room with the painter at night to run through their lines. If she actually had any artistic flair, I can't say, and obviously there'd never been an Assumpção in show business before. But I was happy for her at any rate: it was time my daughter forgot her mourning a little. She couldn't continue with no occupation or objective in life in her forties. And she practised voice control, and gargled, and became all upset when the painter decided to premier the play in Chile, where audiences were more politically aware. There was a protest theatre festival in Santiago, and Maria Eulália used the last of her savings to finance the company's fares. But she was replaced at the last minute by a professional actress, and she was lucky, because just after that all hell broke loose in that country. And when I heard about the arrests of politicians, proletarians, students and even theatre actors, I feared for Matilde's dresses, sensing that I would never see them again. Bad luck, grumbled Maria Eulália, the madwoman's dresses bring bad luck. My daughter had acquired a tic of talking to herself in her days of memorizing monologues. And her grandson always thought she was talking to him, and burbled back at her, and followed her everywhere. The little one did everything he could to get her attention, but she wasn't interested, not even when he started to turn black. Overnight his hair became curly, his nose became even more bulbous, and the darker the boy got, the more I was disturbed by the feeling that I knew his face from somewhere. It was strange because apart from black Balbino and the odd servant or two, I didn't have much contact with coloured people, nor had I ever set eyes on the boy's mother, the one with the made-up names. The boy's colour came from her, evidently; I couldn't expect a communist grandson to find himself a blue-blooded girl. But come on, Father, said Maria Eulália, the boy obviously takes after my mulatta mother. I don't know who'd been filling my daughter's head with such wicked slander, Matilde's skin was almost cinnamon, but mulatta never. She had, if anything, some Moorish blood, via her Iberian ancestors, or perhaps some distant indigenous forebears. The only thing the child had inherited from Matilde was her affection for cheap music. If he so much as heard the neighbour's radio he was unable to hold still. He was a clever boy; I got him a scholarship at my old Catholic school. But the day I took him down to enrol, there was a fuss in the head office and a poofy little priest came to apologize, they weren't taking on any more new pupils. I enrolled him in a public school, where he'd have to rub alongside children of all classes, but I made

132

sure he didn't forget his roots. I showed him the photographs in the desk drawer, his great-great-grandfather with the King and Queen of Belgium, his great-great-great-grandfather walking backwards in London, but he wasn't interested in anything old. He'd accompany me to second-hand bookshops to humour me, but he would stand outside with his hands in his pockets. He still didn't have any facial hair when I first realized he was busy watching women on the avenue. And a chill ran down my spine because suddenly, with just a tilt of his head, he was my father reincarnated. He looked at women just as my father used to, not in a covert or lustful, much less a supplicant manner, but with solicitude, as if responding to a call. Women responded with gratitude, and in time began to come knocking for him; it was all that sleeping on the divan in the living room that gave Maria Eulália her hunchback. To the sound of sambas, rumbas, and rock and roll, Eulálio entertained himself in the bedroom with neighbourhood maids, supermarket cashiers; he even had an Asian girlfriend who waited tables in a sushi bar. He also brought home high-school girls. One day I saw him come home with a milk-white girl who smelled nice and had a graceful walk. That time I held a glass to the wall and pressed my ear against it, curious to hear her moans; I wanted to hear their melody. Beneath a drum-beat I could make out her sad, shrill cantilena, which suddenly gave way to guttural cries, fuck me, ride me up the arse, you big black stud! I'm not easily shaken, but as soon as I ran into her I felt compelled to say, your big black stud there is descended from Dom Eulálio Penalva d'Assumpção, counsellor to the Marquês de Pombal. I later chided myself for my intrusion, not least because if I were to judge women by what they said in bed Matilde had been no saint either. And it wasn't every day that girls of my great-grandson's standing turned up on our doorstep. This young lady lived on Copacabana Beach with her grandmother, who didn't take long to communicate her desire that I come over for a cup of tea. And I could hardly believe it when I read on her calling card, under the name Anna R. S. V. P. de Albuquerque, the address of my former chalet. From the window of the neighbouring building, I'd seen my chalet being demolished; I'd watched, shamefaced, as the roof was removed from the bedroom I'd shared with Matilde, I'd seen the first floor cave in, our walls crumble to dust and the foundations hacked up with a pickaxe. A modernist building had gone up in its place, and I thought it considerate of the architect to raise it on pilotis so as not to bury my memories forever. During the time in which I'd lived next door, I'd often strolled under the building's colonnade and waved the janitors over, sometimes suggesting that they sweep up the leaves or scrub the columns clean. But now there was a fence around the building, an intercom, and a petulant doorman asking me who wished to speak to Madame Albuquerque. The Northerner looked me up and down as I passed him; perhaps he'd never seen a gentleman in tweeds before. And when I found myself face-to-face with Madame

Albuquerque, it was only by a miracle that I was able to make out, through a cascade of wrinkles, the features of Anna Regina, Matilde's youngest sister. I enquired after the health of her parents, who had passed on more than thirty years before, and abstained from mentioning her older sisters. I merely observed that her armchair, placed diagonal to the window, was in exactly the same position as the chair in which Matilde used to rock the baby, except eleven stories up. But my sister-in-law wasn't in the mood for chat and, as the maid served the tea, she ordered me, in French, to keep Eulálio away from her granddaughter. She asked if I preferred sugar or sweetener, and said it would be superfluous to explain why. When I got home, I warned Eulálio of the risks of marrying a blood-relative, even though the girl was a distant cousin. But he didn't know what I was talking about; marriage hadn't even crossed his mind. And he was already involved with others, from semi-virgins to women who turned their faces away as they walked through the door, possibly married. Until one night when I picked up the phone on the first ring; I still hadn't given up on hearing back from Colonel Althier. But a senior detective asked if this was the residence of Eulálio d'Assumpção Palumba Junior. I raced over to Motel Tenderly, where my great-grandson lay face down and naked on a nauseatingly smelly carpet. According to the detective, the motel employees had suspected a kidnapping when they saw an attractive woman in her forties drive up in an expensive car with a young man of humble appearance in the passenger seat. They were thinking of calling the police when they heard six shots, and there wasn't enough time to take down the licence plate of the car that sped off. They had rushed to the woman's aid, and imagine their surprise when they found instead the presumed delinquent's body. But there was no need for the detective to claw at my arm, because I wasn't going to move the boy, all I wanted was to wipe the blood off his thick lips with my handkerchief. At the foot of the bed were his clothes, which the investigators had already gone through for drugs, retrieving some loose change, keys, an address book and his ID. Maria Eulália chose not to go with me to Cemitério São João Batista. The gravediggers were in a bad mood, and when the coffin hit the bottom of the grave with a heavy thud, the muffled sound struck me as the end of the Assumpção line. It was fine by me: I'd had enough.

21

But you've missed crucial events in my life. You've been
so slack lately that when you come to assemble my
memoirs they'll be all over the place; no one will be able
to make head nor tail of them. It'll sound crazy if I tell
you I marched into the Palace Hotel in the early hours,
hammered on the Frenchman's door and, in a deranged
voice, shouted, police! The scum opened the door shirtless
and sweaty, with chattering teeth, as if stricken by a bout
of malaria. And at the back of the room, in the red lamplight, I saw my wife lying back with her legs crossed, her
orange dress tossed over a chair. I saw Matilde lying with
blushing cheeks on Dubosc's bed; naked, unmoving, so
exactly as I'd imagined her that perhaps I was still imagining her. Because I must have arrived at the hotel with
a fixed idea in mind, and, entering his room all in a
fluster, had no time to mould it to reality. For in fact, the
lamplight was bluish, and draped over the back of the
chair was a brown shirt. But the figure of the woman all
curled up on one corner of the bed, covering her body

with the bedclothes, pathetically shielding half of her face with the sheet, could only have been Matilde's. Slut, I thought, whore, I thought, reptile, but not whole-heartedly; it was hard to insult my wife without hurting myself even more. My only consolation was the thought that Matilde was no more than a child, who was now pulling up the sheet to hide her eyes and, in so doing, uncovering her tiny feet. A girl from Copacabana who'd never even seen a ship up close, and I, imbecile that I was, had encouraged her, pointing towards the ocean: there goes the Arlanza! The Cap Polonio! The Lutétia! and first thing in the morning she was planning to board the Lutétia arm-in-arm with Dubosc, who, in her eyes, was a gentleman of note, a citizen of the world. I could just see her, wonderstruck at the thought of travelling in a honeymoon cabin, as a false Madame Dubosc, with a permanent seat at the captain's table. She would be exhibited by her lover in the Paris salons, as Tupinambá Indians were at the French court centuries ago; she would enchant the metropolis with her maxixe, her awful French and her exotic beauty. And then there would be the bateaux mouches, the Eiffel Tower, the Mona Lisa, snowflakes; in no time she would imagine that she had seen everything there was to see in life. Then winter would stretch out, the days would grow shorter, and Matilde, a simple soul, would catch herself in the Luxembourg Gardens dreaming of the playground in Copacabana. Instead of enjoying a good play or cabaret, she would retire every night worrying about her daughter, who, on Rio time, would be with her nursemaid on the beach, or going for a goat ride in the square, or being suckled by the wet nurse. And, in reflex, her milk would become even more abundant and more painful to express, her nipples chapped from the cold. And as she squirted her milk into the sink, Matilde could cry her heart out but I doubt the Frenchman would bother to go to her aid. Once his initial enthusiasm had passed, Dubosc would no doubt prove to be a miserly lover, stingy with caresses and embraces, and overly formal even in bed. But it wouldn't be easy for him either, to live with a woman who whistled to attract waiters' attention, leapt over the turnstile in the metro and insisted on bathing every day. When the Company sent him on a new posting, to a country with a complicated language and strange customs, with enigmatic women, Dubosc would realize that it was time to repatriate his Brazilian. And Matilde wouldn't mind returning from her frivolous adventure in third class, confident that her husband would promptly forgive her. She would re-establish order in the house from the moment she walked in, oversee a spring clean, silence wagging tongues in the kitchen and let the wet nurse go. Little Eulália wouldn't be put out by the change of breast; the greedy little thing would feed as if her mother had merely changed her scent again. And as she nursed her, Matilde would chuckle to herself as she imagined me missing running my tongue around her wet nipples. But, I must admit, I'd gone off milk the moment I saw it splattered around the edge of the sink, its yellowy traces coagulating on the white porcelain, its souring smell. I stopped for a moment to consider that mystery, and when I went to ask Matilde for an explanation, I didn't find her in her room. I then convinced myself that she had raced off after her daughter to make the most of her unexpected milk; Matilde was the kind of woman who would breastfeed in the middle of the square. But she wasn't in the square or anywhere else, and I speculated on my own deep into the night. Because Matilde was never one to venture out alone at night, and soon the baby would wake up hungry. And it was inconceivable to me that her mother should deny her the milk she had in such abundance that she had to pour it down the sink. I don't even know where she kept it all; she didn't have big breasts. But even covered, their exuberance could be divined in a glance, as Dubosc can tell you. On the beach, he didn't take his eyes off my wife's chest, nor was he shy about following her whenever she took the baby into the house. It was either a bladder that needed emptying or drinks that required refreshing: everything was a pretext for him to contemplate Matilde's round breasts as she breastfed Eulália without ceremony in the middle of the sitting room. I bet that's how their affair started; Dubosc in rapture at the sight of the surprising whiteness of Matilde's breasts, rising from such a tanned chest. Hence his visits to the chalet behind my back, when he was surely both praising and forward with her. He wouldn't have given her any respite, putting down to childish wilfulness her refusal to reveal the pair of jewels that he'd already appreciated in other circumstances. To end the harassment, I imagine that one day Matilde finally agreed to open her blouse for him in a corner of the sitting room. And voilà; it wasn't so much trouble to satisfy the rather lascivious Frenchman, old enough to be her father, who, for a few seconds, gazed exclusively at her candid, round, expressive breasts. Matilde was proud of them, and wouldn't have seen any harm in showing them off once or twice more, nor would she have been able to prevent him lightly touching them from time to time to confirm their consistency. And before she knew it, she was shaking with fear, pressed up against the wall under the stairs, being kissed around her breasts, trying to preserve the honour of her erect nipples. But after ceding them, she no longer had any way to decline invitations to intimate visits to the Palace Hotel. Dubosc had travelled through the Orient, frequented brothels in Burma and Siam; he surely was able to manipulate breasts using skills with which I was unfamiliar. In so doing he got my wife addicted, and she no longer waited for invitations to breathlessly slip out of the house for more and more afternoon encounters. And perhaps on her return she felt unworthy of her daughter; she couldn't offer her a breast that had been so slobbered over. Or maybe she'd already fallen pregnant to the Frenchman, and from the outset had reserved her breast for his child's lips. And around the house she wore the dismal ankle-length, long-sleeved dresses my mother had given her to keep herself immaculate from me, seeing as her fidelity was now to a possessive lover. And the hotel staff didn't dare intercept me; it was clear that I would bowl over anyone in my way. I'd kick down the Frenchman's door with the momentum of my arrival. I'd kick down the door of a bank safe if I had to, in the way that alcoholics open bottles with their teeth, in the way that alcoholics long for alcohol with anger; that was how I arrived. I hammered on his door, cried police, and the scum greeted me quaking; I thrust his massive body aside with just one hand. I saw Matilde at the back of the room, covering her head with the sheet; as if I didn't recognize the dirty soles of her beach-going feet. As if I didn't know that the Lutétia was to set sail that Saturday morning, and that she planned to board arm-in-arm with the Frenchman, a gentleman of note, a citizen of the world. I flew at my wife, determined to drag her home by the hair, as she was, naked, to humiliate her in front of the hotel doormen and the drunks on the avenue. I yanked off the sheet in which she had wrapped herself and found the doctor's wife. I had been so certain I was ex-posing Matilde, and it was with repulsion that I laid eyes on the flabby flesh of the doctor's wife. She put her hands over her face, whimpering, and the Frenchman called me savage type, species of maniac and lunatic. I was about to answer him rather bluntly, but he didn't deserve it; the chap wasn't in my league. He was a braggart, a phoney, a man to whom Matilde most certainly would not sur-render herself. An individual who took advantage of a woman with sagging breasts for the pleasure of cheating on his best friend. Matilde needed to know: I'd wake her up to tell her how I'd caught them in the act, but she still wasn't home when I got back. So I lay back on the sofa, closed my eyes and listened to the sea, as I did every night until I dozed off; as Matilde and I had done when we woke from our first night together; I'd never slept on the beachfront before. And from then on I associated one thing with the other; Matilde's breathing summoned the waves, which answered her by rolling up the beach. Spending a night without Matilde seemed as improbable to me as all of the waves suddenly stopping. But suddenly I heard a resounding thud, as if the sea were knocking at my door, and when I opened my eyes, it was dawn. I went outside and the beach wasn't there anymore, the water had covered the sand and the waves were breaking against the pavement, sending up enormous fans of spray. They were making so much noise that I was slow to register a mud-splattered car that pulled up honking at my gate. It was the doctor, whom I invited in reluctantly; it was hardly the hour to be making visits and I already had enough of my own of problems. And he asked me for a drink to boot, his eyes bloodshot; he'd obviously been up all night. He must have been driving around town like a madman and the last thing I needed was for him to think his wife was with me. But no, he had come to say goodbye and thank me for my hospitality, as he was to set sail on the Lutétia that morning. And he would be heading for Constantinople, from where news was arriving of an epidemic of typhoid fever. Besides which, Eva was dying

143

to see the Middle East, he said. Eva had been crazy about Venezuela, Eva had loved Guatemala, Eva had been head over heels for Paraguay; he always said that were it up to Eva, they would have settled down in any one of those holes. He took a sip of cognac and said, Eva's really going to miss Brazil. He apologized for stopping by in such a rush like that, but unforeseen factors had brought forward his departure, and it had been a long drive back that night on rough country roads. Dubosc was going to get a filthy Citroën with no suspension, he said with a crooked smile, but for the miserable fifty million réis he had paid, he couldn't complain. The doctor kept glancing at his watch, saying it was high time he got going, making as if he were about to leave yet not leaving; he seemed to be dancing around an awkward subject. I think he knew all too well who his wife had been sleeping with, as he must have known in Panama, French Guiana and goodness knows where else, as he would know in Turkey and wherever else they went. He dragged her from one place to the next as if she had an incurable disease; but I had nothing to do with his life. I would have hated it if he had chosen me to be his confidant, if he had started confiding in me his woes as he stared into my eyes; I can't bear that kind of thing. But as soon as little Eulália started bawling upstairs, he threw back the rest of his cognac, looked me square in the face and said he was confident Matilde would return to health without any further problems. He'd just returned from admitting her to a sanatorium in a mountainous region with a dry climate, where his public health colleagues would pay her special attention, segregated from low-born patients. He said she had resisted accepting treatment until the last day, but you must have heard this story before. With age, we tend to repeat old memories, and the ones we least like to revisit are the ones that stick in our minds with the greatest clarity. Now I need my anaesthetic; my chest pains have become worse again. I don't think I'll make it through the night. If there's a priest around, have him come and take my confession, as I've been sinning since the day I met my wife. I don't know if I ever told you how I sinned in thought even at church, back in the days when I still went to Mass, but I've been baptized and am entitled to the last rites. I really am inclined to believe in eternal life and have faith that Matilde is waiting for me, though they never explained the resurrection of the flesh properly at Sunday school. Because I was once a dashing young man, and it doesn't seem fair that I should cross over into eternity all decrepit like this, beside an adolescent Matilde. Though I'm not sure what state she was in when she went, because she didn't want to be seen and refused to have visitors. According to the doctor, Matilde made him swear on the Bible that he wouldn't tell me where she was, but this passage doesn't need to be in my memoirs, as it deals with uncertain facts that I didn't witness. When I heard the news I felt dizzy, spent days prostrated, cried a lot, had a fever, night sweats, coughing fits; in horror I convinced myself that I too had lungs full of bacilli. But later I began to doubt the doctor's story, because I didn't remember Matilde coughing, and the laundress would have told me if she'd been hacking up blood. I had my reservations about the doctor, not because he was a Jew, but because he was pusillanimous; his wife could easily have convinced him to tell me a cock and bull story. Eva had been a bad influence on Matilde; she had filled her head with fantasies from the start. She'd most certainly told her about her youth in the Paris of the belle époque, with a complaisant husband and no children to bother her. And now, after forty well-lived years, it's possible that for want of a daughter she saw herself in my wife; the way she looked at Matilde on the beach, at the splendour of her body as she emerged from the water, didn't escape my notice. Eva would happily have agreed to cover up a love affair of Matilde's, and that suspicion made me spring up out of bed. I preferred a thousand times over to roam the city, glimpsing her silhouette in every skyscraper window, than to picture her locked up in a sanatorium. I was bound to run into her one day, even if it were many years later, even if she were kissing another man. And if one day I found Matilde with another man, I'd stare at him more than at Matilde; I needed to know who he was to give substance to my jealousy. I thought about him constantly, dreamed about him many a night, but when I woke I was unable to give him a human form. I could hardly hate a man who hadn't offended my honour, set foot in my house, smoked my cigars or violated my wife. And little by little I found myself willing to accept him; I tried to imagine him as a delicate soul, someone who would watch over Matilde in my absence. I imagined a man who spoke to her only with words I'd never used; who was careful to touch her skin where I'd never touched it. A man who lay with her without taking my place, a man who was happy to be whatever I wasn't. Such that Matilde would think of me whenever she glanced around him, and in dreams would see both of us at the same time, unable to tell who was shadowing whom. And when she woke, perhaps she'd have only a vague recollection of having dreamed of the black-and-white waves in the mosaic on the Copacabana beach promenade. The promenade where she once skipped as if playing hopscotch, because she couldn't step on any stones but the white ones. And where I now hobbled, staggering, because if my foot so much as brushed the black ones, I'd fall into hell. I think hell was Matilde's disease.

22

Such is life. My time had to come sooner or later. Please take care when you move me, gentlemen, as I have a fracture in my femur that hasn't fully healed. Threatening my fellow patients on the ward will get you nowhere. Nobody here will intercede on my behalf. My father is dead, but my mother has money in the bank and family assets. I know her phone number by heart; it's my childhood number. Ask the operator for south 1403. One of you lot will need to speak French, though; in Portuguese, Mother will refuse to answer you. I also have a daughter, my sole heiress; she already had me place my whole estate in her name so as to speed up probate. But Maria Eulália won't shell out a penny for me, not even if you gentlemen send her my ear through the post. She doesn't have anywhere to take it from at any rate, as she recently transferred her inheritance to my great-great-grandson. You gentlemen might even know him: Eulálio d'Assumpção Palumba III, a bit of a Romeo, blond wavy hair; Maria Eulália thinks his blue eyes are reminiscent of my grandfather's in an oil painting that got lost somewhere. Just between you and me, I have my doubts about the legitimacy of the lad, said to be my great-grandson Eulálio's posthumous son. You gentlemen are going to be bowled over, but my great-grandson was as black as your gang leader over there. He had a fling with the mother of the child, a refined young lady, whose word I can't vouch for. But we gave her the benefit of the doubt and raised the child, who was delivered to us as a newborn by Madam Anna Regina de Souza Vidal Pires de Albuquerque's private chauffeur. This sister-in-law of mine is the widow of a sugar-mill owner, former governor of the state of Pernambuco, and lives on the Copacabana beachfront in an apartment full of works of art, baroque saints and gilded shrines. I have her calling card somewhere, but I really can't see her paying my ransom willingly. I don't have a credit card or chequebook, but I'm due to receive a pile of money in compensation for the expropriation of my farm at the foot of the mountains. We can come to a reasonable financial arrangement, maybe fifty-fifty, just as soon as the bureaucrats release the funds. In the meantime, I don't mind being confined, so long as I have a room with a bathroom at my disposal, plus a supply of cigarettes. I'm a light eater, and any kidnapper's hideout will have better food than this hospital. I won't contact the police, I won't cry for help, and I'm obviously in no condition to try to escape. Be advised, however, that if anyone lays so much as a finger on me, they'll have to answer to my great-

great-grandson Eulálio. He set fire to his school for much
less when he was a boy, and after a stint in a reform school
he became even more hot-tempered. But he's always
been his great-grandmother's precious boy; she used to
spend her days combing his curls, afraid they might frizz
up. And she shrugged when I told her the scoundrel had
been stealing from me, because one day I'd be paid back
with interest. I don't know what great future she envis-
aged for the child, who was already a strapping young
man of my size and he still hadn't even finished primary
school. But she argued that he needed money to invest in
his personal appearance so that he'd be accepted in circles
of well-born youths. Foreseeing my own destitution, I cut
all superfluous household expenditure and didn't put my
wallet down, even when I slept. Even so, he continued to
buy leather jackets, phosphorescent tennis shoes, and was
always turning up with the latest mobile phone. With a
bee in my bonnet, I went to Matilde's nightstand and, just
as I had expected, her jewellery was gone. I was outraged,
and my daughter actually had the gall to tell me that her
mother's diamonds were nothing but cheap beads.
Besides which, said Maria Eulália, it's so tacky to hoard a
suicide's baubles in a drawer. I don't know where she got
such a blasphemous idea; maybe she'd looked at the
letters the doctor had written me from abroad. In one, if
memory serves me, he did mention that Matilde had considered an extreme solution at one stage, when she discovered how seriously ill she was. But she drowned that
night because the weather went crazy, the sea filled up in

a second and huge waves would have swallowed any incautious soul who happened to be on the beach. That's what I told Maria Eulália and, as I tried to make eye-contact with her, I told her of the days I spent keeping watch by the seashore, of how I was startled all night long by every wave that crashed. And I confessed that I preferred that Matilde remain ensnared forever at the bottom of the sea to her body washing up on the beach, with goodness what mutilations. And, as a gesture, I had her name engraved on the mausoleum my mother had had built for my father, following the design of a Genoese memorial sculptor. Mother would also be interred there, along with my great-grandson, and I too had a compart-ment set aside for whenever God decided to call me. But the last time I went to Cemitério São João Batista, in the place where the Assumpção mausoleum had been, I found a lilac marble eyesore inhabited by a dead man with a Turkish surname. It was cruel of my daughter; if she had sold our apartment instead of the mausoleum, I'd feel less displaced. And I don't know how many times I've asked you to place me gently on the stretcher; my back is covered in boils. After my check-up, the doctor over in tomography, who strikes me as a young man of a certain standing, will surely have me transferred to a private room, because I'm not coming back to this slum. The people here make fun of my good manners and my correct use of the language offends them. I feel great animosity in the air. Not to mention that some new wretch checks in every day, and the place is in need of ventilation; it's starting to stink. Wait till my great-great-grandson finds out how I'm treated here; he set fire to a nightclub in Ipanema for much less. By that time, he wasn't living with us any more; he'd rented an apartment near his rich friends, for whom he was performing some services. He was even photographed with this party crowd and the pictures appeared in magazines. My daughter cut them out and piled them up on the desk, on top of my family mementos. It was precisely this pile I was sorting through the day Eulálio walked in with a girlfriend named Kim. With a short skirt, bare midriff and a metal ring through her bellybutton, she was an extroverted brunette; she gave me a kiss on each cheek and said, hey. She sat on the arm of my chair and was amused by my photographs. Jesus Christ was tattooed in gothic letters just over her coccyx. She thought it was a magicians' conference when she saw my father wearing a top hat with ministers and ambassadors at the centennial exhibition to celebrate Brazil's independence. So I explained that Father had been the most influential politician of the Old Republic. I told her how King Albert used to come from Belgium to seek his advice, and in one photo I even pointed out Queen Elisabeth and said she was my mother. And when, on an impulse, I told her that the Imperial palace was my family's summer home, she whistled and said, sweet! I was on a roll and would have said more if Eulálio hadn't hurried her along; he'd only stopped by to raid my wardrobe for scarves, gloves, my cashmere cardigan and a Prince of Wales jacket of my father's. He was going to Europe on business, and for the life of me I couldn't work out what language he'd communicate in if he didn't even speak Portuguese properly. But the girl Kim knew a bit of English, and Eulálio had travelled with her on several occasions to Paris, Madrid, Amsterdam; he made good commission on his sales. He always brought souvenirs for his great-grandmother, was affectionate with her and took her out in his new Japanese suv. And she would look at me victoriously, because the boy really did seem to be getting his act together; he planned to marry Kim just as soon as he had saved enough money to buy a beachside apartment in Barra da Tijuca. Kim had her eye on a two-story penthouse big enough for the whole family; she thought it absurd that I should live with my daughter in such a dodgy building, in an area with no prestige. She was shocked to learn that we didn't even have health insurance and made Eulálio pay for a year's coverage up front. It was the most expensive plan around, given the advanced age of its users. He made a point of showing me the receipt and the advertisement; we would have VIP treatment in the best hospitals, even if only to afford us a dignified death. Maria Eulália really had been quite poorly of late; she was a strange colour and her spine was getting more and more crooked. And perhaps sensing her time was near, she made arrangements to donate our apartment to her great-grandson. That was when Eulálio decided to take out a loan and go into business for himself, using his connections with suppliers in Brazil and clients overseas. The whole thing struck me as somewhat nebulous, but Maria Eulália thought the boy was following in the footsteps of my father, who, in the good old days, had made millions of pounds sterling exporting coffee. And on the eve of his next trip, Eulálio surprised me with a box of Cuban cigars; he must have guessed that El Rey del Mundo was Senator Assumpção's brand. I was about to ask after the girl Kim, when the lights suddenly went out and she appeared holding a cake, her black eyes sparkling, her face lit by three candles that formed a 100. I didn't even know it was my birthday, but she planted a kiss on each of my cheeks and handed me a Château Margaux from 1989, the year she was born. Eulálio was talkative; he congratulated me on my hundred-year life of adventures and assured the girl Kim that I had slept with the best women of my time. Now, now, I said, now, now. He did, he said. Grandpa hooked up with Miss Brazils, Hollywood hotties and pulled every high-society fox, bunny and kitten in town. Maybe he still hooks up with them, said the girl Kim, winking at me, and all I could say was, now, now. Not to mention coke, said Eulálio, which you used to be able to get at the chemist's in the old days if you had the cash. It wasn't that talc that any dipshit can get hold of. With that, he had me sit at the table with him and pulled an ebony case out of his suit jacket. I was dumbfounded; I hadn't seen my father's ebony case in the longest time. With my father's mini-spatula he chopped and separated the powder into four hearty lines, handed me the silver straw and said, go for it, Grandpa. And I did, in a single snort; it was much easier to inhale the coke than blow out the candles on my cake. Stop, Father, said my daughter, you'll have a bad turn. In her dreams; I immediately changed nostril and snorted my second line. I'd have snorted all four if the girl Kim hadn't stolen the straw from my fingers. She leaned over me to get to the case, and below the Jesus Christ tattoo I saw the crack of her magnificent arse. And through the armhole of her T-shirt I could see her right breast all the way to her brown nipple; the girl with the caramel skin had a breast as white as cocaine. And just as her boyfriend went for the last line, she pulled up her hair to show me the tattoo on her neck, where it said Eulálio inside a heart pierced by an arrow. She smiled and winked at me. She must have been kidding; I couldn't believe the tattoo was for me. Eulálio suddenly banged on the table and got up to leave; I'm not sure if he was upset about something. I protested, the girl Kim still hadn't had any cake, but then she played the saint and said goodbye to me with a dry kiss on the forehead. Eulálio reassured his great-grandmother, who sighed, full of foreboding, and left, ignoring my request for a ride in his SUV. I hadn't been out of the apartment in a while, and no sooner had the old girl retired to her room, than I decided to get some air, find an open bar with interesting people. When I found myself staring at the deserted street, I headed for some lights in a square, but after a block and a half of walking I was a little tired. I kept on going to the corner, where a police radio patrol car was parked, with two uniforms asleep in reclined seats. Oy! I shouted, thumping the side of the car, and the one behind the wheel woke up with a start and pointed his gun at me. They exchanged glances when I demanded that they let me into the car; I needed to put my legs up before I went on. Installed in the back seat, I challenged them to guess my age, and they looked sceptical when I told them it was my hundredth birthday. One hundred, I insisted, and in excellent health, despite my momentarily racing heart, and I told them about my incestuous love for a young thing born in 1989. Seeing as how no one pursued this topic, I asked them if they were happy here or if they intended to go back to Africa. I said that, in my opinion, serving on the police force was a big step forward for Negroes, whom the government had only employed in public sanitation until just the other day. Then I asked if they happened to know the price of cocaine in Rio, and if possible abroad too, but they were still drowsy. So I asked them to lend me a mobile so I could ask an acquaintance, but the one behind the wheel started the engine and asked where I lived. He drove the wrong way up the street to the door of my building, and they didn't want to come up to have some cake. I had them walk me to the lift, and upstairs I stumbled into bed, where I spent hours talking to myself with bulging eyes and numb legs. I didn't have the energy to get out of bed for the next few days, nor could I keep down the fried eggs my daughter served me. I was bedridden for over a month and lost a good few pounds. It was a long time before I was able to stand up properly, but Maria Eulália thought it would be silly to call a doctor. She was increasingly nervous, shuffling about in her slippers, shaking every time the phone rang, and when it wasn't a wrong number, it was health insurance brokers. One day there was a knock at the door, and I thought the guy in a suit with no tie, his shirt buttoned up to the collar, holding a black briefcase, was yet another salesman. He introduced himself as Pastor Adelton; he'd come to see the property Eulálio had promised him as collateral on an unpaid loan. Get out of my house, sir, said Maria Eulália, but the pastor took the title deed out of his briefcase and strolled through the apartment, examining it carefully. Out, exclaimed Maria Eulália, while I rifled through my desk looking for my lawyer's phone number. Pastor Adelton eventually took pity on us and said he was a man of God first and a loan shark second. And trusting in God that brother Eulálio would soon reappear, safe and prosperous, he offered us a temporary roof. It was a one-room house attached to his church on the outskirts of the city, modest accommodation certainly, but decent. At a glance he figured there'd be enough room for my double bed and, with a bit of skill, the baroque desk I refused to part with. He took it upon himself to have the furniture moved, and even hired a van to transport us with our suitcases and bundles of clothes. Maria Eulália was uncooperative; she had to be forced into the van and sulked all the way there. I tried to distract her by pointing at the mountains on the horizon, the same landscape we would see when we left the city to go riding on the farm, with Maria Eulália in her mother's belly. The difference was that there was no end to the city around us any more; a sea of crude brick houses with untiled roofs sprawled where previously there had been country clubs and nice estates. Bewildered, Maria Eulália stared at the men in shorts at the roadside, pregnant girls with their bellies hanging out, boys racing across the motorway after balls. Those are poor people, I explained, but my daughter thought that they could at least go to the trouble of whitewashing their houses and planting some orchids. Orchids might not survive in that hard earth, and the heat in the van only got worse when I opened the window. We turned off the highway onto a dusty road, and the driver asked a transvestite if he knew where Pastor Adelton's church was. We were told to follow the road until the curve of the ditch. The ditch was a river so muddy it was almost stagnant; as it moved it looked as if it were dragging its filthy banks along with it. It was a putrid river, but I still thought it had a certain charm at the point where it made its bend, in the particular manner of that bend; I think a bend is a river's gesture. And that was how I recognized it, as one sometimes recognizes in an old man a childhood tic, only slower. It was the stream on my farm at the foot of the mountains. And a mango tree on the bank looked so familiar that I almost heard black Balbino high in its branches: hey Lalá, do you want mangoes, Lalá? Further along, the yellow house, with the words Third Temple Church written across the facade, had probably been built over the ruins of the chapel that the Cardinal Archbishop

159

had blessed in eighteen hundred and something. And as I entered the hut next to the church, it comforted me somewhat to know that under my feet was the cemetery where my grandfather had been laid to rest. If one day I came to pass away there, I'd gladly keep him company, since I was partial to that earth, and I even did my best to become accustomed to the miasma from the ditch. The hard part was waking up every morning to the sound of the church loudspeaker, with its prayers and singing. But I wasn't going to be the one to complain if Maria Eulália didn't. On the contrary; it wasn't long before she started attending the three daily services herself. She, of all people, who'd never cared for music. One day I heard her crooning in the outhouse, her voice weak: God is power, God is power. I also noticed that she started discreetly making herself up with pink lipstick and a touch of rouge for the evening service, when Pastor Adelton came to preach in person. And it was on one such night that I remembered the girl Kim's wine, the bottle rolled up in clothes in my suitcase. For want of a corkscrew, I used a screwdriver to stuff the cork down into the neck of the bottle. Wine squirted up in my face, and it's just as well that Mother wasn't there to see me drinking Bordeaux out of a jam jar. Although a little warm, it was a wine with a fruity aroma, one to be savoured blissfully, but I had to finish it before the service ended because Maria Eulália had banned alcohol from the house. Since tobacco wasn't tolerated there either, I put on my velvet robe and went into the yard to smoke my El Rey del Mundo, a cigar worthy of a Château Margaux. The night was humid; over the loudspeaker Pastor Adelton was talking about hell, and although I was sweating heavily I entertained myself by walking around in circles, only taking care not to trip over a mongrel dog that followed me by walking in front of me. Each time I stopped to take a sip of wine, it started to scratch at the ground; a little deeper and it would exhume my grandfather's bones, and his slave Balbino's to boot. And when I flicked away the cigar butt, the dog almost bolted after it but, sensing I was going to the outhouse, it went inside and sat there waiting for me. The darkness of the cubicle spared me the displeasure of seeing my body naked; I swayed as I tried to catch the trickle of water that dripped from the pipe in no particular direction. Slightly giddy, the taste of the wine still alive in my mouth, I concluded that I had got carried away imagining a romance with the girl Kim. It was obvious that I was no longer a man for a girl like that; I wouldn't even dare undress in her presence. And she no doubt slept in the nude with the lights on; she'd go about the house naked all day just to humiliate me. She would take endless showers, callously showing off her perky breasts, her magnificent bottom, her most intimate tattoos. And, as I imagined her bathing for me, I was unable to think of any other scenario but the spacious, sparkling bathroom of my chalet in Copacabana. I have travelled the wide world, gentlemen; I have seen sublime landscapes, artistic masterpieces, cathedrals, but in the end my eyes have no memory more vivid than some

161

seahorses on my bathroom tiles. And as I remembered them, thinking about the girl Kim, I happened to recover the image of my wife, because at that moment the shadow of Matilde lathering her hair fell across the tiles. And her face was already slowly recomposing in my memory, as though a fogged mirror was now demisting. Soon I would be marvelling at Matilde in all her plenitude, her white breasts, her black curls, her thighs with their perfectly brown, unblemished skin. I had actually forgotten that her eyes slanted slightly, and I suddenly thought of those Muslim women who martyred themselves so as to be more beautiful and desirable for their husbands in the afterlife. For your arrows have sunk into me, sang the faithful, and your hand has come down upon me. The dog yelped at my feet, as I remembered Matilde beckoning me towards the tiled wall, walking backwards with softly swaying hips. And then I relived a feeling I'd had as a boy, the first times women had caught my eye, the way they walked, the movement of their skirts, the bulges and depressions in their skirts. As a boy, I didn't understand what was going on with my body at those moments. I was ashamed of what I felt, as if another boy's body was growing inside mine. And now I was slow to catch my own eye, to believe that my desire could be restored at this stage in my life, as strong as it was back when Matilde used to look at me as if I was the biggest man in the world. But yes, I was the king of the world again, I was almost my father, and I threw myself against the unfinished wall as if Matilde were there for me to lean on. I embraced the rough wall, rubbed up against it, flayed myself on it with abandon, and remembered Matilde trembling from head to toe. At one point I even heard her voice, a little husky: I'm coming, Eulálio. Then I slipped on the cement, and before I fell I heard a crack and felt the pain of a bone separating from its marrow. As I lay on the ground I saw my right leg twisted around. There is no soundness in my flesh, sang the faithful, and all I had was a dog to listen to me as I wailed. But instead of barking to alert a neighbour, the stupid thing started licking my face. Inert, I no longer felt any pain at all. I think I actually fell asleep on the wet floor, and I got a fright when my daughter pushed open the bathroom door. The ambulance only came when the sun was up: no one ventures into those parts at night.

23

When I got out of here, I was going to ask her to marry me, but she doesn't want me any more. She gives my stretcher a wide berth and ignores my pleas; she must be tired of hearing me call her by the wrong name. Maybe she doesn't believe I'm going to make it home; I hear rumours that I'm in a queue for a place in a public hospital. Or maybe she's already taken a fancy to someone else in there, some good-for-nothing who bamboozles her, forging memories more fanciful than mine. These sleepless nights are the result; I have no one to give me sleeping pills, painkillers, cortisone. In the beginning I was furious with the stretcher-bearers for leaving me stranded like this in the corridor; they must have been on strike again. But as the days went by I convinced myself that I'm no worse off among all this traffic than I had been in the ward, where the TV was always tuned to the football and I was unable to concentrate on my own affairs. The atmosphere kept getting worse as we received the overflow from Emergency: patients with disfigured faces, burns, amputated legs, bullets in their heads. They were young men, in general, and ill mannered; no sooner had I opened my mouth than they would start: yeah right, Grandpa, and pigs fly! But if with age we tend to repeat certain stories, it's not senility, but because certain stories don't stop happening in us until the end of our lives. Here, at least, I get a bit of attention; there isn't a passer-by who doesn't slow down to take a look at me, like an accident on the edge of a highway. And many hang back to listen to my words, even if they don't grasp their meaning, even when my emphysema suffocates me and I wheeze more than I speak. On Sundays, at the peak of visiting hours, whole families will often gather to appreciate my death rattles, or perhaps hear the last sentence of a dying man. I have invoked Death on many an occasion, it's true, but when the actual moment arrives for me to see him up close, I trust he will hold his scythe aloft until I finish telling the story of my existence. So I start to recapitulate my family's most remote origins, and there are records of a Dr Eulálio Ximenez d'Assumpção, alchemist and private physician to Manuel I of Portugal, in fourteen hundred and something. I descend at a leisurely pace to the threshold of the twentieth century, but before I enter my own life, I make a point of revisiting my ancestors on my mother's side, a branch of Indian hunters in São Paulo State, and another of Scottish warriors of Clan Mackenzie. Until not long ago I was spelling these names out to a nurse, who left me after she'd wrung my memories dry. But that's what she

166

thinks. I'll have you know, ladies and gentlemen, that of my wife alone, I still have a trunk full of untouched memories in my head. I don't know if I ever told you people how I met Matilde at my father's memorial service; maybe it's worth arranging to have my depositions recorded. If it weren't for the tremors and cramps in my hands, I'd fill a notebook, in minute calligraphy, for every day I spent with my wife. After she left, however, my days would consist of much paper and little ink, drawn-out and lacking in event. Until the morning in which I received a letter from Dr Blaubaum, from Constantinople, in a Hotel Divan envelope. Eva had fallen in love with Constantinople, etc., etc., typhoid was spreading through Asia Minor, etc., etc., and it was only in the last few lines that the doctor mentioned Matilde: despite the grim news he'd been receiving, he hadn't lost faith in her full recovery, thanks to his colleagues' diligence and the mercy of God, etc., etc. On an impulse I took my car and drove up into the mountains, where I knocked on the doors of countless sanatoriums, charitable institutions, farming colonies, and even wound up at an asylum. But even if I investigated every hospital in the state's interior, it would be impossible to locate a patient who'd been admitted under an assumed name, a patient of whom I didn't even have a photograph. On my way back down to Rio, I began to fill with rage at that foreigner who had appointed himself my wife's guardian, when he couldn't even look after his own. That was more or less what I told him in a telegram that was returned to me; the addressee wasn't a guest at the Hotel Divan any more. Thinking he may have tired of his nomadic lifestyle, I took advantage of my last visit to Paris to try to track him down, at the city hall, at the gendarmerie, at the telephone company. But apparently Dr Blaubaum no longer kept a residence in the city, where I imagine Eva had already given him enough headaches since the years of the belle époque. And when I returned to Brazil, although I didn't find Matilde waiting for me with open arms, there were also no alarming letters on my bedside table. No news, good news, I thought on my way to my mother's place, where I'd report to her on our financial troubles. She was having afternoon tea with the parish priest of the Church of the Candelária. I heard voices in the winter garden: the poor, my mother was saying, she caught a disease of the poor. I'm not sure if Mother had already begun to confuse her words at that stage, but immediately the priest corrected her: not of the poor, Maria Violeta, it was the disease of lust that was her undoing. There was obviously new gossip about Matilde going around town. As soon as she had left me, people started whispering behind my back, at the grocer's, at the coffee shop, at the barber's; I know they were speculating about my wife's possible lovers. But they fell into a profound silence when I arrived, as if I'd been promoted to a respectable category of deceived husband. Or fearsome, judging from the behaviour of two of Matilde's former classmates, who, in their haste to avoid me, crossed Avenida Nossa Senhora de Copacabana and boarded a moving tram. All I had wanted to do was to invite them round; maybe it would have encouraged Matilde to come out of the room she had holed herself up in. But I'm already making a muddle of things. Matilde wasn't in the house any more, and the house without her became a shambles; the staff had taken off while I was away. The only one left was the nursemaid Balbina, who stopped taking little Eulália out because, in the square, on the beach, wherever she went, people told her the baby should be locked away with her mother, or put in quarantine. I also preferred not to show my face on the street and kept to myself, preserving myself for my great revenge. Because when Matilde returned to our chalet, the whole neighbourhood would hear maxixes and sambas coming from her phonograph. She would take the baby to the square herself, breastfeed her while sitting on the swing, greet the nursemaids and new mothers with her breast out, and laugh for no reason. On Copacabana Beach she'd walk beside me so everyone could see her in a bathing suit: an adulteress, maybe, but healthy and flawless in body. So I waited for her at my bedroom window every night, and Matilde didn't come, didn't come; Matilde had never missed our furtive encounters. And just when I was about to lose all hope, she would steal onto the lawn on tiptoes, and I'd hurry downstairs with my heart in my mouth to open the kitchen door for her. And she would lean against the kitchen wall, opening her black eyes wide, but maybe this scene is from before we were even married, and not from the time of the things I was talking about. It's not my fault if events sometimes come to mind out of the order in which they took place. It's as if, following the example of Dr Blaubaum's letters, some memories are still coming by ship, while others have already arrived by airmail. And it was on airmail paper, as fine as rice paper, that a letter arrived for me from Senegal one day. Eva was already adapting to Africa, after the intense cold in Indochina, etc., etc., and although productive, their stay in Indochina would always be overshadowed by the news of Matilde's tragic disappearance, Matilde's tragic disappearance, tragic disappearance, always overshadowed by the news of Matilde's tragic disappearance. The doctor apologized for the tone of his previous letter, which he had written in the heat of the moment, his emotions at a boil, saying that he prayed constantly for Matilde's tragic disappearance, disappearance, prayed constantly for Matilde's soul, yours affectionately, Daniel Blaubaum. The previous letter arrived from Indochina long after the letter from Africa that mentioned Matilde's tragic disappearance. By that time I thought it had been lost at sea; I didn't think it existed any more when it arrived. It was a fat letter, in an envelope from the Hôtel Caravelle in Saigon and bore a postage stamp showing a Chinese junk at sea. I gazed at the boat with its large bamboo sail, franked with the date 29-12-29. I turned the envelope over; it was closed with a ruby seal. I checked the name of the sender, D. B. I weighed the letter in my hand and guessed there were at least eight pages in there, with writing on both sides, in the doctor's dreadful scrawl. I re-examined the pumpkin-coloured two-piastre stamp; it must have been cheap. I picked at the edges of the ruby seal with my fingernail; it was like scratching a scab. I held the envelope up to the light, entirely opaque, and the fact that I never opened it will sound cowardly. Perhaps I should have tried to learn about my wife's suffering from the start, find out what malady the doctor had seen in her that, living under the same roof, I hadn't, find out if he had examined her with a stethoscope right there in our house, if he had asked her to undress, if he had confirmed his suspicions, if he had communicated his diagnosis to her frankly, without camouflaging it with medical jargon, or with scientific terms in French, and if she had understood everything right away regardless, if she had cried, if she had asked him if she was going to die young, if she was going to die ugly, if she had asked God what would become of her daughter, if she'd had a kind word to say about me. Perhaps another man in my place would have got into the car when he finished reading, taking in his pocket the letter with the address in the mountains, and when he got there he would have visited her room and bed, gathered up her clothes, her shoes, thanked the people who had helped her, asked about her last days, how desperate she was, how she looked, how much she weighed, in which shallow grave she was buried. But by leaving the letter intact in its sealed envelope, I believe that I respected the wishes of Matilde, who wanted to slip out of my life as cats disappear, ashamed to die in front of their owners. And for that very reason I perpetuated her name without her, engraved on the mausoleum in the eclectic style of achitecture that my mother had had built for my father. I only touched that letter again years later, briefly, as I transferred all of the doctor's correspondence into a drawer with a lock in the desk I had inherited from my mother. There were something like a dozen letters from different countries, not all of them opened, some half-read, as well as cards of season's greetings that used to arrive sometime around Lent. Then a postcard from Algeria, which I received in 1940, a year after it had been sent, and I never received another word from Dr Blaubaum. It was better that way, since another world war had broken out, our government was hesitating to take sides, and my correspondence with a Hebrew might have been misinterpreted. Especially now that I aspired to a position of responsibility in the public service, seeing as how Mother's allowance wasn't keeping pace with inflation; I had even had to sell my car. I had been thinking about Matilde's father, who, according to my mother, had even managed to weasel his way into President Getúlio Vargas's entourage. My political differences with my father-in-law were no longer of significance, to my mind, since under the new regime Congress had been shut down and our political parties no longer existed. And to show I didn't hold anything against him for old family squabbles either, I swung by little Eulália's school in a taxi on my way to the Catete Palace, so I could present her to her grandfather in the uniform that would remind him of his late daughter. It wasn't the first time I'd been to the palace; I'd been there with my father as a teenager and had spent hours playing in the gardens with President Artur Bernardes's children. That's why I burst out laughing when an employee with an Indian jawline told me that Deputy Vidal wouldn't see me without an appointment. I tossed my calling card on his desk, repeated my name syllable by syllable, to which he responded, big fucking deal, while my daughter complained about missing lunch, and in the middle of all this kerfuffle I heard a voice boom, good afternoon, Lilico. And I bristled, because the affectionate nickname my father had given me sounded like mockery from anyone else's lips. But it was Matilde's father, who was waving at me as he walked past, flanked by a group of men carrying piles of papers. Good to see you, he said, in passing, and when he had already passed me he added: give my regards to Maria Hortênsia, getting my mother's name wrong. I followed him through the hall, dragging little Eulália, who decided to dig in her heels. Deputy Vidal, Deputy Vidal; at the bottom of a flight of stairs he finally turned to listen to me. I announced my willingness to consider his old proposal again, but before I'd finished my sentence he pointed at Eulália, is that your daughter? It's your granddaughter, sir. Maria Eulália Vidal d'Assumpção is Matilde's daughter. What a delightful child, said the deputy, and handed her a packet of rock sugar he had in his pocket. But Matilde, Matilde, he said, and I noticed he had the same perplexed air as the

173

mother superior, like someone looking for the glasses they've forgotten on top of their own head. Ah, yes, Matilde, a coloured girl we brought up as if she were one of the family, and with that he turned to climb the stairs and one of his lackeys barred my way. Just as well Eulália was busy with the rock candy; hearing the children at school say her mother was a beggar was already enough for her. To this day she resents the fact that she never knew Matilde. Although I don't place much faith in such newfangled ideas, sometimes I think my daughter should try psychoanalysis. Maybe that way she would spare me the embarrassment she has subjected me to of late, when she lets fly at the evangelical services, giving personal testimony of her past suffering until the day she found the hand of God. And her suffering always stems from her mother, whom she claims was as vain as Salome and stopped giving her milk so her round breasts wouldn't shrivel. Maria Eulália is gaga; she forgets things she said the day before. The day before she declared in that same pulpit that her mother had died in childbirth like Rachel, Jacob's wife. It would seem her long-term memory is prodigious, however; the other day she said that she remembered the man who, in the middle of the night, came to compete with her for Matilde's breast. She can even recall the smell of alcohol on his breath and the accent of the man, a foreigner who died with her mother when their car overturned on the old highway from Rio to Petrópolis. With equal conviction she announces that her possessed mother threw herself off a bridge, or from

174

an ocean liner, or drowned on a raft that sank, in a fisherman's arms. And my daughter said that it was the fault of this mother, dissolute like the wife of the Prophet Hosea, that she grew up with no friends, receiving prank phonecalls; and worse than being called a whore's daughter was being labelled a leper. She swears before the assembly that when she was a child she had to wear a bell around her neck, and that everyone on the street used to run away from her, because her mother had hanged herself in a leprosarium. And I'm forced to hear these absurdities over the loudspeaker. Maria Eulália exposes her mother to the judgement of the rabble in the church. I mean no offence to simple folk: I know a lot of you are bornagains, and I have nothing against your religion. It may well be a step forward for Negroes, who only the other day were sacrificing animals in Candomblé rituals, to be going about now all dressed up with the Bible tucked under their arms. I have nothing against the Negro race either; I'll have you know that my grandfather was a leading abolitionist. If it weren't for him, you might all be getting beaten about the head to this day. With the possible exception of this pallid lady, who I know from somewhere; talk of the Devil, it's my daughter. Come and give me a kiss. You're growing more hunched by the day; be careful not to drop the baby. If you say that this Eulálio is the boy's son, I'll take your word for it, but I sense that the features of an Assumpção will soon be like those of an extinct species. He must take after his mother's family, with whose origins I'm not familiar; I don't even know

the girl's surname. That's if the mother is the girl with
the tattoos, because the lad liked to play the field; he
may even have planted his seed in a married woman, or
that Japanese girl who never left our apartment. I know
he had a son with Matilde's sister's milk-white granddaughter, but that's not him. You must be confusing him
with the baby who was born in the army hospital. That
one's already fully grown; it seems he knocked up a girl
with a made-up name, but I honestly can't keep track of
all these youngsters that have started to be born in more
recent years. On the other hand, I can recall every strand
of hair in my mother's bun. I haven't seen my mother in
a while, but I think she came to take my temperature; I
do hope she sings me a berceuse. I didn't recognize her
before because of the baby; I'd never seen my mother
holding a baby before. It's not surprising: I was an only
child and Mother never picked up anyone except me, and
even then only once in a while. If I started whinging, she
would hand me over to the governess, who'd hand me
over to the nursemaid, who'd hand me over to the wet
nurse for her to breastfeed me. With effort I can even
remember seeing myself clinging to her, in the mansion's
Venetian mirrors, but I don't know what Mother would
be doing with me in a pestilent environment like this.
However, I'm now having a vague recollection of her
taking me when I was still a baby to say goodbye to an
old guy, if I'm not mistaken my great-great-great-grandfather, who was lying on his deathbed in a field hospital.
The famous General Assumpção must have been about

176

two hundred years old: he looked older than Methuselah. The century before last he'd fought Robespierre and now he lay prostrate on a simple litter. He was no longer making any sense, claimed to be Afonso VI of Portugal's chamberlain and thought he was in the Palácio de Sintra in sixteen hundred and something or other. I felt sorry for him because he only had Mother and I to watch over him. I was surprised that no officials or field marshals came to see him, not even a representative of the royal family. I only saw strangers around him, some rough-looking individuals who laughed at him. And more gathered around when he opened his eyes wide, turned purple and lost his voice; he wanted to speak and nothing came out. Then a young nurse pushed through the crowd, bent over my great-great-great-grandfather, took his hands, and whispered something in his ear, which calmed him. Afterwards, she passed her fingers lightly over his eyelids, and covered his once handsome face with a sheet.

Note on the Author

Born in Brazil in 1944, Chico Buarque is a singer, gui-
tarist, composer, dramatist, writer and poet. Although he
first made his name as a musician, in 1968 Buarque was
imprisoned by the Brazilian dictatorship for writing and
composing the existential play *Roda Viva*. During the
1970s and 1980s, he collaborated with other artists in
protest against the dictatorship. He is the author of
numerous novels; in 2010 *Spilt Milk* (*Leite Derramado*)
won both of Brazil's leading literary prizes, the Prêmio
Jabuti and the Prêmio Portugal Telecom. He lives in Rio
de Janeiro.